PULSE POINT

COLLEEN NELSON
and NANCY CHAPPELL-POLLACK

yellow dog

Yellow Dog
(an imprint of Great Plains Publications)
1173 Wolseley Avenue
Winnipeg, MB R3G 1H1
www.greatplains.mb.ca

Great Plains Publications gratefully acknowledges the financial support provided for its publishing program by the Government of Canada through the Canada Book Fund; the Canada Council for the Arts; the Province of Manitoba through the Book Publishing Tax Credit and the Book Publisher Marketing Assistance Program; and the Manitoba Arts Council.

Design & Typography by Relish New Brand Experience
Printed in Canada by Friesens

Library and Archives Canada Cataloguing in Publication

Nelson, Colleen, author
    Pulse point / Colleen Nelson & Nancy Chappell-Pollack.

Issued in print and electronic formats.
ISBN 978-1-927855-97-3 (softcover).--ISBN 978-1-927855-98-0 (EPUB).--ISBN 978-1-927855-99-7 (Kindle)

    I. Chappell-Pollack, Nancy, author II. Title.

PS8627.E555P85 2018   jC813'.6   C2017-907263-3
                                               C2017-907264-1

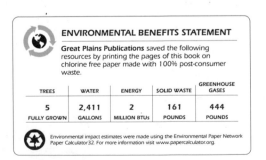

ENVIRONMENTAL BENEFITS STATEMENT

Great Plains Publications saved the following resources by printing the pages of this book on chlorine free paper made with 100% post-consumer waste.

TREES	WATER	ENERGY	SOLID WASTE	GREENHOUSE GASES
5	2,411	2	161	444
FULLY GROWN	GALLONS	MILLION BTUs	POUNDS	POUNDS

Environmental impact estimates were made using the Environmental Paper Network Paper Calculator 32. For more information visit www.papercalculator.org.

Canadä

FSC
www.fsc.org
MIX
Paper from responsible sources
FSC® C016245

To Oriyen,

PULSE POINT

Thanks for coming to
the MYRCA launch!
NOP

Enjoy reading!
♡ Collin.

For Mitchell, Shane, Talia and Casey Pollack

Kaia

I was lean, we all were. Mae told me about the plumpness of bodies before. It sounded so funny, to think of bodies jiggling, a layer of fat coating muscles. The only thing I could pinch between my fingers was skin. This was how bodies were meant to be in the City: efficient machines. The gymnasium was busy, as it always was in the morning. Citizens were eager to earn joules to take them through the day. I took my spot on a running mat beside a woman who walked with plodding, determined steps. Her sunken cheeks puffed out with effort. Droplets of sweat fell to her tight-fitting running suit and were immediately absorbed.

As I ran, I watched the digital display on my finger climb past 70 to 80 and then over 90. If I rubbed my thumb against my forefinger, I could feel the small, raised bump, a microchip that had been implanted at birth. Every Citizen had a pulse point; it connected us and monitored the energy we used and the energy we created. 'Energy in equals energy out' was the chant we lived by. Equilibrium was essential to maintain the safety and security of the City.

I could feel someone watching me and looked up to the balcony. Wearing his uniform, a grey tunic still stiff with newness, stood an overseer with a hint of a grin on his face. I resisted the urge to smile back. Lev should know better. The overseers had important jobs in the City. They were the Council's right hands, ensuring order was maintained. The Lev I knew was anything but an enforcer. He'd sworn to me that he wouldn't take his role as seriously as some of the others did. I wanted to believe him, but up there with his hands clasped behind his back, shoulders and spine set, he looked like the rest of them. Except for the slight curve of his mouth when his eyes fell on me.

There was one other thing that marked him as different. A large stain, as big as a handprint, stretched across his left cheek. He kept that side of his face turned away from the gymnasium. A superficial defect, it had gone unnoticed on the genetic screenings before he was born. He wasn't a defective, but he was less than perfect to some Citizens, who shied away from him. It had never bothered me; maybe because I had blue eyes, another rarity in the City. We'd been friends for as long as I could remember.

From up above, he winked at me and my stomach fluttered. I gave a slight shake of my head, a warning for him to get back to work. I loved the attention, but if another overseer caught him, he'd get reprimanded, no matter who his birth elder was.

The woman beside me slowed her pace as I sped up. She checked the numbers glowing through the skin on her index finger. Satisfied, she stepped off her mat. I wondered how long she'd been on it. I'd reach my minimum joules in under an hour, but I'd keep going. I'd share the extra energy I accumulated with Mae. As I ran, my core muscles tightened, the momentum of my legs effortless, my breath coming in short, economical bursts. I looked over. Beside me someone else had taken the place of the woman.

"When did you get here?" Sari asked, grinning. Her blond hair, long enough to be harvested and used for fertilizer or woven into fabric, was tied up. I'd miss her hair. Mine had been recently cut.

Unlike Sari's, it was short and fine, curling a little at the temples, I didn't miss the weight of the long hair. But Sari's hair was something else. It usually hung in a golden sheet down her back.

"A few minutes ago."

"Long enough to see Lev?" she teased.

I lifted my eyes to the balcony. A different overseer watched us, older and stern-looking. Behind him, through the transparent, solar-panelled dome, the sky glowed fiery orange and clouds pooled in the distance, brewing a storm.

"Still hoping you'll be matched with him?"

I never should have shared my secret with her, I thought with a twinge of regret. "No, because it'll never happen." A defensive tone crept into my voice, which only annoyed me more. As the offspring of a female who'd died young, my genetic ranking would be too low to match with an overseer. Even though Lev was marked, he was progeny of Kellan, the legendary overseer, and Tar, a Councillor, making him a top pick for a mate.

"Never know," she sang out.

It was second nature to glance at someone's fingertip. As much information could be learned from it as the expression on their face. Sari's energy level was already high. Why was she at the gymnasium? She caught my look and gave me a guilty one in return. "I can keep my hair a while longer if I energy share," she said, averting her eyes.

I shook my head at the thought of the corrupt overseer who was willing to take energy in exchange for bending the rules. Her hair was long past harvesting length. If someone on the Council noticed, they'd ask questions. It was dangerous for both of them. But vanity was Sari's downfall; the admiring glances of others was too tempting to ignore. More than once, I'd seen her pink her lips and cheeks with berry juice. Even now, as her hair fell out of its tie, she let it wave behind her as she ran.

"Once I've been matched, I'll cut it off," she promised. Her words came out in quick bursts as she ran.

"How much are you giving him?" Deals for energy didn't usually favour the seller.

"Her," she corrected. "Thirty joules."

"A day!" I stumbled on my mat and looked up, the overseer had moved on. "That's crazy!" I hissed.

Sari's cheeks had grown rosy with exertion, or shame. "My profile went up twenty-three days ago. The only options I've been given were a wastewater engineer, a storeroom supervisor and gardener apprentice." She shot me a look, and I knew in Sari's mind, those would never do. "Someone suitable has to show up soon, right?" She stopped running and looked at me, desperate for agreement.

What she wanted was an overseer, or a surgeon, maybe a Councillor's offspring; someone with some status. Sari had put her name up for matching as soon as it was allowed, but I was in no hurry. She thought it was because of Lev, that I was waiting for him to be matched first. But that wasn't the real reason, at least not all of it.

Both of us began running again, our feet pounding in unison. "You just have to be patient," I consoled her. "Strong genetics on both sides, a good job at the clinic," I rattled off all her attributes. "The right match will come along." She brightened a little at my words. I followed her eyes as they glanced at my finger and the glowing number. It was high enough that I almost didn't need to run.

"I'll share some with you, if Mae has enough," I offered, taking pity on her.

She smiled with relief. "Thanks, Kaia."

We didn't speak again, both of us intent on our exercise. Above, clouds collided, hanging low over the dome. The wind turbines spun at a frenzied speed. A bolt of lightning shot to the ground and hit a conductor. The lights in the gymnasium flashed brighter with the surge of energy.

Mae had told me about how the world worked before the City had been built. There had been countries and governments and people had lived in houses without a dome to protect them. For a long time they'd been safe, or at least they *thought* they were safe. Scientists had given warnings about the dangers coming, but no one had listened. The disasters started gradually at first, but then grew in frequency. When the ice caps melted, the ocean levels rose and cities flooded; hurricanes slammed coastlines over and over. Droughts destroyed crops. Forest fires and mudslides forced evacuations and millions were left homeless. People were starving and cities became war zones. Governments crumbled and people turned on each other, battling for food and water. No one thought it would get so bad. No one except the Scientists.

Their warnings had been ignored, so they'd acted on their own, quietly siphoning away research and money to create self-sufficient Cities, like the one I lived in. Run on the energy of its Citizens and sustainable in every way, Cities were safe. But there was a catch. Only people with the right skills and genetics were allowed to live here.

Mae had told me about the early days of the City, when the people who'd been turned away swarmed the dome, desperate to be let in. The stories she told me sounded fantastical. There were beasts, fierce pack animals bred in the City's underland that were able to survive outside. They guarded the dome, ripping people to shreds if they tried to attack.

That had been a long time ago. There were no beasts anymore, at least not around the City. And the people who had begged to be let in had retreated to the Mountain, where they lived a primitive existence, if they lived at all. We called them

Prims. Despite the overseers' insistence that the nearly feral group of City rejects were still a threat, most Citizens were unconcerned. The daily Prim Threat Level we received on our hologram hadn't moved above "low" in years.

By the time I stopped running, 125 glowed through the flesh of my finger. My body radiated heat and the moisture was wicked away by the fabric of my bodysuit. I stepped off the mat and waved goodbye to Sari.

I looked up at the overseer balcony and was surprised to see Councillor Tar, the woman who had birthed Lev, staring back at me. The chill of her gaze made me shudder. Harsh and imperious, it was surprising that Lev shared DNA with her. I didn't like that she was watching me, or the way she narrowed her eyes and tilted her head, as if I'd answered an unasked question.

Lev

Clouds, black with fury, spread out over the horizon. High winds made the panels on the dome undulate. There was always something to see outside in the constantly changing skies. Not like in the City, where everything stayed the same. Same job. Same people. Same day, every day. I stifled a yawn as Raf, my mentor, gave me a stern look, a reminder to keep my eyes on the gymnasium.

Gripping the railing of the balcony, I forced my gaze back to the gymnasium floor. Hundreds of mats were laid out in rows, and the sensors underneath collected the joules created as Citizens walked or ran. The mindless occupation of the City. And me, stuck on the balcony, staring out at the Citizens for the next fifty years.

As I stood up straight, the overseer tunic cut into my neck and sat heavy on my shoulders. I looked longingly at the exercise suits of the males in the gymnasium. Why did overseers have to wear such uncomfortable clothing? To keep us grumpy and miserable, probably.

The irony was that as boring as overseeing was, it was a desirable job. Overseers had esteem, lived in the best dwellings and were given preferential treatment when it came to matching. My cohort in school hadn't understood my glum acceptance when the career placements had been announced. I should have been pleased, but I wasn't. The job was joyless. Other careers in the City brought reward—gardeners grew things, teachers developed young minds, doctors healed. But overseers? All we did was, well, oversee.

Before I could get too lost in my dismal thoughts, Kaia arrived. I drank in the sleek fit of her suit, the curve at the base of her spine and the place where it widened into something slightly softer. And then moved my gaze up to her face; angular cheek bones jutted out against the hollow of her cheek, contrasted by full lips with a slight upturn at the corners. If anyone was to criticize her features, it would be her nose that they'd find wanting: it fell straight, a little too long for her face. No one would fault her eyes though. I was too far away to see them, but their blueness always surprised me. A genetic rarity in the City, but an acceptable one.

I waited for her to glance up.

Her name drummed through my head, anticipation building in my chest.

She raised her chin with exaggerated slowness as if she'd known I was watching her since she'd walked in. Our eyes locked. I started to smile down at her, but she gave a slight shake of her head. A reminder that on-duty overseers were not to engage with Citizens.

I shut my eyes, registering her image in my memory so I could save it for later.

I couldn't resist, when I looked down at her again, I winked, enjoying the blush that crept up her cheeks.

"Lev?" Tar's harsh voice destroyed my moment of peace. I turned to face her. The stubbly hair on her head had grown into dark brown tufts, like a blanket covering her dome-shaped skull. With a pointed nose and slash of eyebrows, the woman who birthed me eighteen years ago looked as menacing as ever. As one of the five Councillors in the City, she wore a scarlet tunic. "What are you doing?"

"Overseeing," I said, wryly.

She took a deep breath, suppressing her annoyance. "Your first balancing is today."

"Today?" The fabric at my neck grew tighter, like it was closing off my windpipe.

Tar frowned. "You are an overseer," she announced, her words crisp. "It's part of your job."

Gritting my teeth, I nodded. *Part of the job you secured for me*, I wanted to add. Unlike me, most Citizens had a say in their career placement, or at the very least were given choices.

With a sigh, she pulled me away from the balcony. Her face softened a little. She dropped her voice to a whisper. "It is not *your* choice to balance. It is the City's, by order of the Council. Do not feel empathy for the balanced, feel pride that you are helping the City keep equilibrium. You are doing the work the Council demands of you."

The Council sat in their underground chamber deciding who lived and died. Balancings came at their orders, but not by their hands. Balancing rid the City of the old and the weak and had been done since the City's inception. I'd grown up knowing one day I too would be balanced. It was the only way to maintain stability and keep our City strong.

But still, my stomach twisted into knots. What if I knew the Citizen? What if they fought, or cried? The City made it sound like there was honour in balancing. A long life lived, and in gratitude, the City killed you.

Another overseer walked behind us, nodded at Tar, and relieved me from duty. Tar turned back to the gymnasium floor, her eyes darting from mat to mat and settling on Kaia. "That's your former classmate, isn't it?" Each pump of Kaia's legs and arms was efficient and graceful.

I kept my face neutral, wary of her sudden interest.

"I've noticed her before. She's strong." Tar nodded at her with appreciation. "She runs for her elder, you know. Mae, an original inhabitant," Tar looked at me, one eyebrow arched. "She's delaying the inevitable. Mae could be balanced at any time now. I looked into her energy production. It's dismal. If her name came up, the Council vote would be unanimous to have her balanced. Kaia's energy could be better used elsewhere."

Tar tilted her head at me, daring me to argue.

I clenched my jaw, doing my best to keep my face neutral. I couldn't let Tar see how much her words rattled me. Why was she looking into Mae's energy production in the first place?

"You should go," she said with a dismissive wave. "Raf will be waiting for you."

With a quick bow of my head, I turned away, grateful to escape. I didn't know if Tar's threat to Mae was real, or if she was trying to manipulate me. Whichever it was would be dangerous. One thing I'd learned was that attracting Tar's attention rarely meant good things were coming for you.

Kaia

Mae had told me that before the City, I would have called her "grandmother," not elder. Sy would have been called my "father" and Raina, long gone, would have been "mother". Such titles didn't serve a purpose in the City, so they'd ceased to exist.

Instead, we referred to children as offspring, and mother and father became birth elders, or progenitors, the true biological terms for what we were to each other. I imagined those terms suited Sy just fine. In the same way Mae was open and loving, Sy was distant and cold. When I was younger, I excused his unresponsiveness as quiet dignity. After all, he had the awesome responsibility of keeping a whole City fed; he never complained that his back ached from planting seedlings or pinching insects, one-by-one, off leaves of kale; or the numbness in his lanky limbs, folded under him for hours as he sank to the ground, careful not to squash tender sprouts.

But as I grew older and met other gardeners, I realized it wasn't the grueling physical work that made Sy withdraw, it was the past.

He never spoke about Raina, but her death was a festering wound, painful and bothersome, that stood between us. Sometimes, at night, I heard him thrashing against the walls of his sleeping capsule, begging her to stay. Asking him questions got me nowhere. He'd clam up and retreat. So it was Mae I went to.

She called up memories and projected them from the pulse point in her fingertip as holograms. Some of them I kept, second-hand, filing them away in my memory chip so I could watch them over and over. Raina had been a surgeon, curious and bright; excelling in academics, she'd gotten in trouble for her endless questions. The memories showed a tiny female with a laugh that burst from her mouth. Her movements were quick and efficient, not plodding like Sy's.

I couldn't replicate her laugh, but I'd tried. I thought bringing part of her back to life would ease Sy's troubled mind. "It doesn't work that way, Kaia," Mae had said. "You'll never be her."

I wasn't smart enough to be a surgeon, so I was sent to the clinic as a fetal assessment technician. It was here, with Sari, that I spent my days bent over a microscope testing embryos for genetic abnormalities. It wasn't until I'd been working for a few months that I realized, after trying so hard to be like Raina, I'd been given a job that had more in common with Sy's. I was a gardener too, tending the crop of future Citizens.

A lineup of females greeted me when I walked in. The clinic's bleak interior, whitewashed adobe walls and floors, was devoid of personality. The constant hum of the pulse piece, spewing information in my ear, was the only sound in the space. I pressed a spot behind my ear and turned it down low; the sudden quiet was disarming. Like an extra limb, the noise of the pulse point was as familiar to me as breathing. But at work, it was also a distraction. I'd get caught up in the latest weather report and ignore a patient's question. With it nearly silent, I could hear the gentle slap of my bare feet on the floor and the way females cleared their throats when we called their names, the little cough belying their nerves.

My stomach clenched when I saw my first patient of the day sitting in the waiting area. I recognized her. Older than me, she'd been in with another pregnancy a few months ago. Lying on the table, she'd told me the names that she'd chosen, her cheeks rosy with excitement. It had only taken a second in the screening room for me to tell that something was wrong with the embryo.

I'd told her as gently as possible, but she'd looked at me as if it were my fault the fetus was defective and it had to be terminated. And now, she was back again.

Her blood filled the vial, swirling in a gush of scarlet. Pale, her mouth pinched with worry, she'd stared at the ceiling until I pressed the vein and pulled out the syringe. I gave her a reassuring glance and left the room to run the first test.

The equipment had been in the City since before. State of the art for the Originals, it showed its age now. The metal was dented and nicked, small blips and static filled the screens. The room was off-limits for anyone but a technician. Did the patients wonder what went on back here, where we determined the viability of the offspring?

Placing a droplet of her blood on a glass slide, I pushed it under the scanner. A warning beep came back almost immediately. My stomach clenched. An aberration. I ran the test again. Same beep. I didn't need to run further tests. It would have to be aborted.

"What's wrong?" Sari whispered when she saw the look on my face.

"It's not viable."

Sari's eyes slid away from my face. She took a deep breath and concentrated on her lab work.

"It'll be her second termination," I told her, frowning. For a moment, I thought about not telling her. What if the baby was born and the abnormalities weren't evident at first? Or maybe never? What if whatever genetic mutation showed up on the test wasn't an issue? Maybe the baby would just have a birthmark like Lev had, or be left-handed. I never knew exactly what was wrong, just that something about the DNA didn't fit within the parameters set out by the Council when the City began.

"You have to tell her," Sari said, reading my hesitation correctly.

I nodded. The City demanded every Citizen contribute. We couldn't be responsible for anyone who was unable to produce energy. The only way for the City to remain efficient was to follow the rules. A fetus showing genetic anomalies must be aborted.

The patient, her skin ashen, sat on the table. I'd been gone longer than normal. She twisted her tunic between her fingers, squeezing her eyes shut and muttering pleas for her unborn child.

The words spilled out of my mouth before I could think about the implications. "Everything looks normal," I said with a forced smile. She gave a sigh of relief, her face lighting up with a grin, oblivious to my wide-eyed amazement at what I had just done.

Swallowing back bile that rose in my throat, I nodded that she could leave. She would be told eventually, probably next month at her appointment. I'd only delayed the inevitable. She'd enjoy four weeks of thinking a healthy offspring grew inside of her. And then? I turned away and went to call the next female.

Since I'd been at the clinic, the storm clouds had opened up. Rain hammered on the exterior walls of the dome, blurring the landscape outside. The stream that ran through the City was already churning with the newly collected water. Sy would be happy. His garden, at the far end of the City, would be well-irrigated.

But seeing the rise in water level, I moved away from the edge of the walkway. Mae had told me that before, people would play in water. Swimming, she called it. I didn't understand how it was enjoyable, to splash the way she explained. My experience with water was short bursts of hot steam in the communal cleaning cubicles. The droplets condensed on my skin and then I wiped them away. There were many things from before that made no sense to me, some of them were funny, but others had been destructive. I was glad I was in a place where those mistakes wouldn't be made again.

Which is why my lie to the female at the clinic that morning was so dangerous. Mae told me defectives used to be born and then cared for. I knew the City couldn't run like that: it wasn't sustainable to care for people who couldn't provide for themselves. So, why had I lied to the female? If an overseer found out what I'd done, I'd be punished and sent to an underland cell. I'd been placed in the clinic because of my personality profile. "A unique ability to show compassion and logic with others" it had read. I hadn't shown either today.

125, the joules I'd earned that morning in the gymnasium, glowed through my skin. I stared at the number. Even after a day of using the City's energy at my workspace? I rubbed my thumb against my finger feeling the raised bump under my skin. Its incessant beat had vanished. How had I not noticed it before?

I paused on the walkway and held up my finger. The small gesture produced a hologram that floated in the air in front of me. I sighed with relief. Maybe I'd imagined the stillness. All the usual information appeared: a weather report; Council bulletins; my energy calculations for the day; and Sy, Lev, Sari and Mae's locations within the City. An icon on the bottom opened the images saved in my memory chip and the current Prim threat level, low, as usual.

I looked at the hologram more closely. Some of the information was wrong. *Clear skies*, it read. *Calm winds*. But outside, the storm raged with no sign of letting up. "Weird," I muttered under my breath. I stared at it a moment longer, then tucked my finger into my palm when two overseers appeared.

Crossing a bridge, I looked towards the Mountain, where the stream entered the City. The water was purified by an ultra-violet light system, and the City relied on a constant supply flowing in and out. I followed the stream towards the terraced dwellings that were made of adobe, like every other structure in the City. The clay was easily repaired and required little energy to produce; it stayed cool, moderating the City's temperature. Each unit had a balcony as big as the dwelling itself filled with rows of hydroponic plants. None was as crowded as ours though. Sy's talents as a gardener ensured that we ate well.

From the walkway, I could see Sy's tall, lean figure hunched over one of the plants. Which Sy would greet me? I wondered. His moods were unpredictable, switching from near manic to apathetic. Some days, he'd sit comatose, refusing food, rousing himself only to go the garden. His energy level had gone dangerously low a few times and I'd had to energy share so he didn't draw the attention of an overseer. I raised my hand in a hesitant wave when he looked down to the walkway. He grinned and held up a bright red tomato, its skin glistening. I breathed out another sigh of relief. For today at least, I had nothing to worry about.

The musky, earthy odour hit me as soon as I walked in, so different from the antiseptic smell of the clinic. In my dwelling, vines snaked around the room and beans dangled from the ceiling. Clusters of tomatoes glistened in hydroponic containers and rows of lettuce bordered the room. Sy grew things in our dwelling that he wasn't allowed to grow in the garden, like strawberries and lemons. Over the years, these plants had been deemed too inefficient, the nutrients they provided to the Citizens not worth the resources they consumed. But Sy had saved the seeds and if he wanted to deplete his joules caring for them, so be it. I wasn't complaining. There was no taste better than a fresh strawberry.

The bright colours jumped out against the adobe walls and bamboo furniture. Like other Citizens, we had only what we needed in our dwelling: a bamboo bench, one low table in the dining area and another, taller table for preparing food. A few pillows sat on the floor for lounging in the sitting area. Our sleeping capsules were down a narrow hall.

Mae stood at the tall table organizing a basket of food she would bring to the communal kitchen. "Sy brought beets home," she said and held them up by the stems, like a prize. "I thought we could make soup."

Mae was a head shorter than me, her short hair shone silvery, and her eyes were still lively and crackling with energy. Wrinkles

nestled into her papery soft skin. As she filled a basket with supplies, I stared at her hands, mesmerized by the gnarled, purplish
veins and bulging knuckles. There were few Citizens as old as
Mae left in the City.

"I'll help," I offered. We piled the beets, along with onions
and garlic into the basket and she picked it up. She'd only gone a
step or two before she gasped. Her forehead furrowed with pain.
"My hip. It hurt too much to exercise today."

"Did you tell Sy?" I asked.

"There's no point in keeping it a secret."

Her pragmatism made my heart lurch. Why couldn't I have
been as practical at the clinic today?

Pulling up my hologram, I swiped my finger to a picture of
Mae, frowning when the locator said she was in the market. With
another swipe, I shared 50 joules with her and glanced at my
finger. It still read 125. "How many joules do you have?" I asked.

"Oh!" she gave a surprised gasp. "Can you spare that much?"

I nodded, ignoring a twinge of guilt. I shouldn't be sharing
energy when my pulse point was broken. But Mae needed the
joules, I reasoned, and it wasn't like I'd stolen them.

The added energy bolstered Mae, and even though she
limped a little, she collected the final supplies for the kitchen
with more vigour. "I'll tell Sy we're going," I said.

He was still on the balcony tending to the plants but looked
up when I joined him. Plucking a grape off the cluster, he rolled it
between his fingers. "Try this." He held it out to me. Soil rimmed
his fingernails, outlining the oval shape. Long and tapered, they
belied the strength hidden beneath the calloused fingers.

Resting the basket against my hip, I took the grape, admiring the plumpness of it and popped it in my mouth. The juice
burst on my tongue, sweet against the bitter skin. "It's good," I
said, swallowing.

"A drought-resistant strand. I think I've got it perfected." He put another one into his mouth, savouring the taste.

From the walkway below, someone called my name. When I looked over the ledge, Sari waved up at me, a basket of supplies in her arms.

"Are you coming?" she called, as if I should have been expecting her.

"To the kitchen?"

"I sent you a message," she said. "After work."

She had? I felt a flicker of worry. I'd never received a message from Sari. Although, she *was* flighty. Maybe she thought she'd sent it and hadn't? I pressed my thumb to my finger, urging my pulse point to start beating, but there was nothing. The little chip inside of me was dead. "Be right there. Mae's coming too."

The storm clouds had turned the sky dark. A subtle glow emanated from the solar lights lining the walkway. Mushroom-shaped umbrellas that captured sunlight during the day, they collapsed into lampposts in the evening. Located between the dwellings and the garden with the field and wastewater pond beyond, the kitchen was a low-walled structure filled with separate workstations for Citizens to use. Each one had a counter, stove and oven, powered by piped-in gas. Along one wall was a trough sink and on the other, compost and vermiculture bins. As usual, it hummed with activity. Mae went to a long table and set out our supplies, while Sari and I found empty cooking stations.

I hesitated before touching my finger to the sensor, worried that it wouldn't start. But gas hissed through the element, ready to be lit. Beside me, Sari was about to do the same, but I waved her hand away. "Let me." Once again, igniting both elements hadn't depleted my joules.

"Thanks," she whispered, tucking an errant strand of hair behind her ear.

"So you sent me a message an hour ago?" I asked.

"Yeah, two actually, when I didn't hear back." She leaned in closer. "Did everything go okay, with the termination?"

I nodded. The kitchen wasn't the place to tell Sari what had really happened. And I wasn't sure I could. I'd broken every rule we had at the clinic.

"I didn't get either of them," I said, frowning. "Have you ever heard of a pulse point malfunctioning?"

Sari put a pot of water on the element and shook her head.

I gave an irritated sigh. "Mine's stuck on yesterday's weather. It's not getting the newsfeed, or messages. And"—I checked to make sure no one was listening—"I don't think it's spending my energy."

"Did you tell an overseer?"

I shook my head.

Sari widened her eyes in surprise. "You haven't told anyone?"

"I only noticed after work," I said with a guilty look. Mae's laugh trilled out from where she worked, her shoulders shaking as she talked with a male elder.

"So, you mean, you could use as much energy as you want and it wouldn't affect your supply?"

I showed her my finger. "The same number as after I ran this morning, nothing's been depleted. I even gave Mae fifty joules."

She raised her eyebrows in disbelief.

I lifted my finger and the hologram appeared. With a few swipes, I shared another fifty joules with her. A second later, the digits on her finger blinked and a new number glowed through her skin, but mine stayed the same.

She gasped and started to giggle. "Kaia!" she exclaimed joyfully, but then quickly became serious. "What if an overseer finds out?"

"Maybe it's just a glitch. It might fix itself."

"I wouldn't blame you if you didn't want it to be fixed. Can you imagine not having to worry about depleting your energy? Not having to run for hours every day?" Even though her words were said in a whisper, I gave her a look of caution as Mae came over, the beets glistening on the cutting board, free of their gritty peels.

"What are you two gossiping about?" Mae teased, dumping the beets into the water to boil.

"Matching," Sari blurted. She threw me a look. "As usual."

"I remember those days," Mae gave her a wistful smile. "Your pot, Sari." It had boiled over and with a gasp of surprise Sari ran to her station. Mae shook her head with a grin. When she turned back to me, her expression grew serious. "So, you'll talk to Sari about matching, but not me?"

Her question stung because we *hadn't* been talking about matching. "You have nothing to worry about," Mae said, forcing me to look at her.

"Yeah, right," I grumbled. Mae had told me about before, when people chose their mates based on love, not genetics. It was such a risk, to let emotion dictate a choice like that. The City had taken away that choice in the first years Citizens lived here.

She clucked her tongue at me. "DNA isn't the only factor in a match, Kaia."

But it was the biggest. And thanks to Raina's early death, potential mates would worry that whatever had killed her would affect me, or could be handed down to offspring. And then there was Sy. We kept his shaky mental state a secret from the overseers, but I couldn't hide it from a mate. What if it got passed on to offspring? Or developed in me as I got older?

"I have genetic anomalies on *both* sides," I whispered. "Who would want me?"

The truth was, it wasn't just the probability of a poor match that bothered me. It was Lev. The thought of losing him to someone else sent pains shooting through my chest.

"The beets are ready," I said, and pulled my hands away, relieved to change the subject. I lifted them, steaming and slick, out of the boiling water. The knife sliced the beets smoothly; their blood-red juice stained the cutting board.

"Don't look so glum, Kaia," Mae said. "You're young. You have so much to look forward to."

I bit back a retort. One day, and I didn't know when, she'd be balanced. My friends would be matched and I would live in a communal house with no mate and no offspring. As far as I could tell, I had nothing to look forward to.

I looked at my finger. 125.

Maybe Sari was right, why draw attention to my pulse point if I didn't have to? I hadn't done anything to break it. Let the overseers figure it out. Until then, I should enjoy my newfound freedom as long as I had it.

Lev

"Guess this is your first balancing," Raf said as we walked up the stairs to the elder's dwelling.

"Yeah. I'm nervous," I said and then regretted admitting it.

I knew Tar hadn't picked Raf to be my mentor because he was a good listener. She'd picked him hoping some of his intensity would rub off on me. Raf was broad-shouldered, with hair cropped close to his scalp. Crevices ran along either side of his mouth, giving him a permanent frown. His lean physique was similar to many males in the City, but there was a toughness to him that only some overseers possessed.

He checked the number on the door against the one on his hologram. A likeness of the elder floated in the air along with his name: Vic. He was nearly bald, with sunken cheeks and skin so pale and thin, the veins in his face showed through. There was no age listed. It didn't matter how old he was, only that he no longer produced energy. Some starved themselves, sitting alone and wasting away, too weak to get help. Better to go this way, I thought, than to have to hide, afraid of the end.

Vic opened the door as soon as Raf knocked. He was small and only came up to Raf's shoulder. He knew why we were there; I could read the resignation on his face. "Will you come with us?" Raf asked, extending his hand. Those were the words we were taught. Make it sound like it is their choice, give them some dignity. The reality was that he had no choice. If he fought, we would give him a jolt with our stun gun.

Vic nodded, loose skin trembling on his neck. I peeked inside the dwelling. It was dim and empty; he'd probably traded his belongings for a few last joules. The plants on his balcony were brown and wilted, long past the hope of producing food.

I opened my mouth to say something, to reassure Vic that he'd made the right choice, but Raf threw me a look. It wasn't our job to put him at ease, so I assumed the same stern expression as we marched along the walkway. Vic was slow, stumbling and leaning on us for support. By the time we arrived at the balancing clinic, Raf and I were almost carrying him.

The room was sterile, empty except for one mat, covered only with a strip of rough hemp cloth and pushed against the wall. The balancer, his thinning hair so blond it disappeared against his pale skin, entered, holding a small bamboo bowl in his hands. He nodded to the mat. Raf and I were to place Vic on it, but his limbs went stiff and refused to bend. Through the transparent skin at his wrist, his pulse beat erratically.

"Hush," the balancer said quietly, nothing more than an exhale as he approached Vic. I shivered at the sound of his voice, but Vic relaxed, his arms hanging limply and his knees buckling. Raf and I positioned him so he sat with his back against the wall. Wrinkling my nose at the odour of urine, I looked down and saw he'd pissed himself. Was that normal? Raf looked unconcerned. Twenty years older than me, he'd probably led a hundred elders to this room.

I pressed Vic's wrist against the floor, gently. I didn't want to break his bones but he needed to be immobilized. Holding his elbow down with my knee, I clenched my teeth and avoided looking at Vic's face. My stomach churned and I tried to think about something else, anything else, than what I was doing.

Raf reached for Vic's chin, dragging it down so his mouth opened. Vic whimpered in fear, his body rattling. I struggled to hold his shoulder to the wall, surprised at the strength of someone who looked so weak.

The balancer crouched down beside him. Despite the pallid colour of his skin, his lips shone red as they twisted into the slightest of smiles. "This will be over soon," he said soothingly. He raised the cup of pulpy juice to Vic's mouth and gave a nod of encouragement. "Freshly squashed white baneberries," he articulated slowly. "You will feel nothing, I promise."

We all waited, the cup poised in front of his mouth. *Drink it*, I silently pleaded.

The balancer tipped the cup and the liquid trickled into Vic's mouth. But instead of swallowing, he spat it out, the poisonous drink spraying over the balancer, white and frothy. Vic thrashed out of my grip. One leg kicked and caught me in the jaw. I screamed with surprise and fell back.

"Idiot!" Raf yelled at me. "Grab him!"

I ignored the ache in my jaw and the heat spreading across my face. The balancer scrambled out of the way, wiping white baneberry juice off his face, and I lunged to secure one of Vic's arms. Raf beat me to it, elbowing me out of the way and pinning the elder down.

"Grab your stun gun!" Raf growled at me. I fumbled for it in its holster. "Never mind," he grunted. "Hold him!" I straddled Vic, taking Raf's place. Vic gnashed his teeth, the tendons on his neck stretched taut as he strained under me.

"This could have been easier," Raf grunted as he pressed down on Vic's throat. I watched as the elder's face turned purple and his lips and eyes swelled. Vic wasn't fighting anymore.

Blood pumped loud between my ears as Vic gasped and choked for air. "Lev!" Raf barked. I tightened my grip, but that wasn't what he wanted. "You do it," he commanded. "Balance him." I looked at him horrified. "Put your hands here," he nodded at Vic's neck.

I shook my head. I couldn't. Balancings were meant to be dignified, the way we were taught in training. This was barbaric!

"Do it!" Raf's voice was a dangerous. "It's an order."

I looked at the elder and then shut my eyes. The balancer came from behind and put his hands where mine were. Raf kept shouting at me and the room spun. I would have run if Raf hadn't grabbed one hand and forced it on Vic's windpipe. His trachea bulged but his pulse was slow. "Both hands," Raf ordered. I did as I was told and squeezed.

And squeezed.

And squeezed.

I kept my eyes shut, counting out Vic's dying pulse until there was nothing.

"He's gone."

Raf pried my hands from the elder's throat and I moved away, shaking. The balancer put his finger on the elder's neck, checking for a pulse I knew wasn't there. Raf rose and grabbed my shoulders, hauling me up. "They're unpredictable. Even the weak ones fight back," he said. "You can't let your guard down. Not for a second!" He gave me a meaningful look. A wave of nausea rolled through me. I leaned against the wall to steady myself. "Take him away," Raf said to the balancer. I thought he was talking about the elder, but it was my arm that the balancer tugged on. "Go back to the gymnasium. Wait for me there," Raf called over his shoulder. I couldn't get out of the balancing room fast enough.

My legs trembled as I made my way to the gymnasium. As soon as Tar found out what had happened, she'd make me do another one. There was no room for weakness, especially in me, the off-spring of a Councillor and Kellan, the City's hero. But whatever robust genetic code they'd passed on had been rearranged into something else. I'd never be the person she wanted me to be.

I made my way into the gymnasium and up to the balcony. I scanned the floor below hoping Kaia would be there, but instead my eyes landed on Mae. The oldest person in the room, she trudged along on the sensor mat. Even from where I stood, I could tell her hip bothered her. She held it and winced with each step. No matter how much energy Kaia shared with her, she wouldn't be able to avoid a balancing much longer. Vomit rose in my throat thinking about Mae's life ending the same way as Vic's.

From the corner of my eye, I saw Tar approach. Gritting my teeth, I focused on the Citizens below, losing myself in the relentless pounding on the mats. "Lev." Her voice was like a slap. "Come with me."

I wanted to shake my head and tell her to leave me be. I should have ignored Raf's orders and gone to my dwelling. The last thing I needed right now was her reprimand. But she gestured for another overseer to take my place on the balcony and shot me a withering glare. To defy her would mean punishment. I had no choice.

We descended to the walkway and followed the stream, not in a relaxed stroll, but with purpose. Tar had a long stride and her arms swung at her sides. At the sight of her scarlet tunic, Citizens darted out of the way, bowing with deference as she sliced through them.

Tar led me across a bridge over the field: rows of rice, the thin, reedy stalks steeped in water would soon be harvested. Insects were more plentiful in the garden and fields, so we kept birds to regulate their population and pollinate the plants. All small, the birds flitted, filling the space with their high-pitched songs. A bright yellow one with green feathers on its wings flew low and then darted through the door that Tar held open for me.

I hesitated, wondering why she'd brought me to the aviary. Tar nodded for me to enter. Two dead trees, left over from before, stood tall and gnarled in the centre. Nests sat in the crooks of branches and knotholes, birds twittered and called to each other.

Tar closed the gate after her. Its clang sent down a flurry of activity and downy feathers. "Come here," Tar said. She'd stopped beside one of the trees. What was left of the bark was covered with layers and layers of splotchy, white bird droppings. The ammonia smell burned my nostrils, but Tar wasn't bothered by it.

She pointed to a nest, compact and the size of her palm. Within it, three newly hatched birds. Without feathers, their miniscule organs and veins glowed through translucent skin. Eyes closed, newly formed beaks opened instinctively, calling with silent tweets for food.

"They only hatched yesterday," Tar told me, her voice a hushed whisper.

I looked at her, surprised.

"I come here often. It calms me," she said in answer to my unasked question. She turned back to the nest. "They're totally helpless." She reached into the nest and pulled out a bird. Its claws dug into her finger. "Raf informed me of the balancing."

I bowed my head as shame and guilt spread through me.

"It's hard being an overseer and it wasn't your first choice of a career; I know that." Tar held the bird up close to her, peering at its helpless form in her hand. "But balance has to be maintained. It might seem harsh, but the City depends on it." She paused, waiting for me to look up. When I did, her brown eyes burrowed into mine.

"To show weakness, remorse, *empathy*," she shook her head, "to the elders will only weaken us. The City began with strict rules. It is up to us to enforce them. With a population of three thousand, how many elders do you think the City can support? Ten? Twenty? A *hundred*? And who determines who they are? Can you think of what would happen if every Citizen wanted their elder spared from balancing?" She shook her head. "There are only so many lives the City can support."

I followed her gaze to the bird on her palm. She closed her fist around the body, the tendons in her hand bulging as she squeezed. When she opened her hand, the bird lay lifeless on her palm.

I stared at her. My gut rolled with nausea.

"I don't want to hear about another incident like today." She dropped the dead bird at the foot of the tree amongst a mound of discarded feathers. She tilted her head, as though appraising me. An unfamiliar brightness filled her eyes. "The City is changing. The Citizens need a leader. One leader." I stood frozen when she reached up to trace the contour of my cheek, her fingers cool. "It will be me. And when my time is up, the role will pass to you. Your future in the City could be secure, but you have to want it. You have to show others that you are willing to make the hard choices. The choices other people can't make."

I stood motionless in front of her.

"Be who you were meant to be, Lev. Be a leader," she said in a dangerous whisper.

Every piece of me wanted to scream the truth at her. I would never be the person she wanted me to be. I wasn't her. I wasn't Kellan. I wasn't a leader.

But all I could do was nod.

The female bird returned, dropping food into the mouths of her babies. The two survivors fought over a worm that was deposited in the nest, oblivious to their sibling lying in a mangled heap on the ground below.

Kaia

The Sy of yesterday, so excited about the feel and taste of the grape, was gone when I returned to our dwelling after work. He didn't acknowledge me when I joined him on the balcony. Instead, he stared at the Mountain in the distance, quietly mumbling to himself.

I hated when he slipped away from us, but it was better than when he flew into rages, shouting that he'd do it all differently if he had the chance, that he'd made a mistake. He wanted Raina to come back. Mae was the only one who could calm him down. She'd whisper that it wasn't his fault. Raina was gone and there was nothing anybody could have done to help her.

We should have reported him to an overseer. His unpredictability made him if not dangerous, then at least a concern to the City. But if we did, we were condemning him to balancing. And the truth about my genetics would be revealed: deficiencies on both sides. No, our lives were intertwined. My survival in the City depended on his.

Backing away from the balcony, I collected everything I needed to prepare dinner. He continued to stare, oblivious to my presence.

"Kaia? Sy?" Mae burst in, a damp sheen of sweat clung to her face. She'd been to the gymnasium, even though I'd told her it wasn't necessary. I had enough energy to share with her.

"Did you see it?" she asked, breathless. Her eyes were filled with worry, eyebrows drawn together.

"See what?" I asked, shaking my head. After work, I'd made one stop at the market, and then came back to the dwelling. A glistening pot of honey sat on the counter. A special treat for Mae, we'd dip Sy's strawberries in it later and lick it off our fingers. Though it was worth as much energy as some people produced in a day, its purchase had depleted none of my joules.

"The Council's news!" she hissed, casting a furtive look at Sy. She waited for me to pull up my hologram and read it for myself, but if I did, she'd see that it was malfunctioning. What if she insisted I tell an overseer?

I'd been careful not to draw attention to myself, although the honey had been an extravagance. That morning, I'd run for an hour and a half, enjoying the sensation of running because I wanted to, not because I had to. Having unlimited energy allowed me to help Sari and Mae; I wasn't being selfish or indulgent. As long as I didn't arouse suspicion by doing anything stupid, why did I have to tell anyone?

"Can't you just tell me? I want to get dinner ready." I grabbed some fresh vegetables out of the basket and fussed with utensils, hoping to look busy enough that she'd let me off the hook.

"Energy sharing has been suspended."

Her words caught me off guard and the squash I held slipped out of my hands. It hit the floor with a sickening thud. "What?" I couldn't have heard her correctly.

"It was sent out as I left the gymnasium. I thought you would have seen it." She peered at me. News like this would have spread through the City in a matter of minutes. Of course, she'd think it was strange that I hadn't heard.

"But, that means..." the reality was too horrible to say out loud. Without energy sharing, every elder was in danger of balancing. "Why?"

Mae shut her eyes and winced, one hand flying to her hip.

"Because they can," she said, bitterness lacing her words. When she opened her eyes, they were wet with tears.

I pulled Mae into a hug. She rested her cheek on my shoulder. Her thin frame shook with silent sobs, her grey hair soft against my chin. I glanced to the balcony where Sy stood, still staring at the Mountain. Had he heard the Council news? Is that why he'd slipped away?

Living with a broken pulse point had left me stranded in my own City. What else had I missed? But telling an overseer now would mean admitting I hadn't reported it right away. The thrill of having unlimited joules had blinded me to the dangers of being disconnected. I couldn't think about any of that right now though. All that mattered was Mae. And holding her tighter, I wondered what I would do without her.

"I'll talk to Lev. Maybe he knows what's going on, or can speak to Councillor Tar for us. Maybe they can make an exception." Even as the words left my mouth, I knew they sounded naive. Lev held no sway with Tar.

But they gave Mae some hope. She pulled away from me and nodded, wiping her eyes. "I always thought I'd take the news better. All these years," her voice cracked. "I knew the day would come, but I still don't feel ready to go."

Clutching her hands, I held them to me and blinked back tears. I wasn't ready for her to go either. "Lev can help," I said with more confidence than I felt.

◠

Locating Lev proved harder than I expected. The two-day-old reports in my ear were useless, so I silenced them. But without the constant banter, I felt like my head was in a dome of its own. Everyone moved around me with knowledge that I didn't have. I'd been born in the City, yet without my pulse point to call up at a moment's notice, I was lost. I had no way to locate Lev, except to search the spots he might be.

First I went to the gymnasium, then to his dwelling, but he was at neither. Shaking my head in annoyance, I realized that if I wanted to find him, I'd have to ask for help. A somber mood hung over the Citizens in the kitchen. They worked silently with none of the usual chatter. "Sari," I whispered a greeting. "I need your help. I have to find Lev."

Even Sari's bright eyes looked dull. "You heard," she said, frowning.

I nodded. "I'm worried about Mae. I need to talk to him."

"It's still broken?" she whispered. I wasn't sure if it was jealousy or judgement in her voice.

I swallowed back a retort. She was the one bribing an overseer so she could keep her hair. "I can't tell anyone now." And it was true. As long as Mae was in danger, I needed to be able to give her as many joules as possible.

Sari hesitated and for a second I thought she wasn't going to tell me where Lev was.

"Where is he?" I pressed.

"In the orchard," she said.

I turned to go, but she leaned in close, tugging on my arm.

"Do you think the new rule is because of me? My deal with the overseer? Maybe someone found out." She'd braided her hair and tucked the tail into the neck of her tunic, hiding it. "If the matchmakers found out, it would hurt my chances of finding a good mate," her voice dropped. "They'd wonder about my *questionable morals*."

She wasn't thinking about Mae or any of the elders. All she cared about was finding a mate. "This has nothing to do with you," I told her.

"Are you sure?"

If she noticed my thin-lipped nod of annoyance, she didn't say anything. I wished Sari had a second-degree ancestor. Maybe then she'd understand the tenderness I felt for Mae and how scary the new energy-sharing rule was to me. But I wasn't in the mood to explain it to her. Without saying a proper goodbye to her, I left the kitchen. Let her worry about her hair and being matched if those were the things that mattered to her. Mae was what mattered to me, and no one was going to take her away from me without a fight.

Between the garden and the field lay the orchard. Rows of trees hung heavy with blossoms or fruit depending on the time of year. A figure sat underneath an orange tree, his head resting against the trunk, legs splayed in front of him. Lev heard me approach and looked over, his face relaxed when he saw it was me. "I thought you hadn't got my message," he said.

I almost told him about my pulse point, and then stopped. Not because I didn't trust him; I did. But if I told him and then it was discovered he'd kept it a secret…I cringed at the punishment that would be given to him. Anyway, a broken pulse point was trivial compared to helping Mae. I'd deal with one problem at a time.

"I got away as soon as I could," I said, pacing. I couldn't sit down, I was too worked up. It didn't help that I kept hoping my pulse point was going to suddenly start working.

"Kaia," he said and stood up. He didn't have to say anything else. He put his hands on my shoulders to still me. "It'll be okay."

I gave him a look of disbelief. "No, it won't."

He frowned and was about to say something, but instead dropped his hands. Someone was on the path walking towards us. I darted out of sight behind the tree. It wasn't technically a punishable offence to be together, but we both knew it put us in a tricky situation. The Council made it clear that emotion couldn't be allowed to dictate matches, and it was why every Citizen's hormones were regulated through their pulse points. But neither of those things had stopped us from meeting before.

As soon as the Citizen was gone, I sank to the ground. Lev sat down beside me. My skin tingled where we touched. As usual, having Lev so close made me forget the warnings about romantic entanglements. What had begun as a childhood friendship between Lev and me had developed into something more. We met like this often, escaping to private corners of the City. I got a bittersweet tumble in my stomach being so close to him, every minute cherished because it would all come to an end when he was matched.

Today was different though.

"Lev, the energy-sharing rule," I broke off and looked at him helplessly. "Why are they doing this?"

His expression turned grim. "It's a culling. They've done it before, ridding the City of the weak," he said, his voice low.

"Mae will be one of the first to go, won't she?" Panic rose in me and my voice trembled. "Can you help? You're one of them now. You have power."

"Kaia—" he started, shaking his head. "I can't argue with a Council order."

"Tar brought it forward, didn't she?"

"I don't know," he said, but I knew I was right. I could read it on his face.

"I thought overseers and the Council were supposed to protect us," I fumed. "But instead they attack the weak. It's not fair." I looked at Lev, hoping to incite a reaction.

"Nothing about the City is fair." His voice was hopeless as he stared off at the Mountain. "I balanced someone yesterday."

My chest ached for what that must have been like for him. Anyone but Tar could see he wasn't meant to be an overseer. "Was it horrible?"

"He fought. I didn't think he'd be so strong." Lev turned his unmarked cheek to me. A purplish bruise coloured it.

"Oh, Lev," I reached for his hand and held it in mine. He closed his eyes and his chin quivered. For the hundredth time since he'd been assigned overseer, I wished he could stand up to Tar and tell her overseeing wasn't for him.

"I would have let him go, Kaia," he said. "We didn't have to end his life. Not like that."

I thought of the female at the clinic, the one with the non-viable embryo. I'd let her go, making a choice that had nothing to do with the good of the City. "Go to the Council. Tell them you want to be reassigned."

Clutching his arm, I felt his muscles tense. He shook his head. "Do you know how hard Tar worked to get me assigned as an overseer? She had the career analyst rewrite my placement report."

I stared at him in shock. I hadn't known that.

"I thought after yesterday she'd see, I'm not like her, or Kellan. But it didn't make a difference. She thinks one day I'll take over the City," he said with a mirthless laugh. "That I'll be a leader." Lev shook his head. "She has no idea who I really am. I can't spend the rest of my life balancing elders." He pressed the heels of his hands against his eyes. Without energy sharing, there'd be more balancings, many more.

A lump grew in my throat thinking about Mae spending her last moments in a dark room with an overseer and a balancer. If she was taken when I was at work, I wouldn't even have a chance to say goodbye.

"I wish we could leave," he blurted. "How could outside be worse than it is in here?" He looked back towards the Mountain. "We could go together." He squeezed my hand and met my eyes with a melancholy smile. "To the Mountain and beg the Prims to take us in."

"What about the beasts?" I asked.

"We'd tame them, or run fast." He gave me a wry smile, then shifted so his body was facing me.

"And then we'd live there, free from everything and make a life together."

"Yes," His word was a whisper, his breath licking my earlobes. I was powerless against him as his hand snaked its way up my arm, cradling the back of my head.

"Lev," I moaned. His lips brushed mine and my heart beat wildly. What we were doing was wrong, every nerve screamed it, but how could I make him stop when I didn't want him to?

But he did. He always did because we both knew the consequences. Forcing ourselves apart, I adjusted my tunic and lay back down beside him, nestled in his arms.

"I could never leave Mae," I whispered.

He nodded. "She could come with us."

I tilted my head and saw him smile.

"I'll ask her," I said, playing along. It was an impossible dream, we both knew that. No one could survive outside the City.

Lev grew serious. "I'll talk to Tar tomorrow. Maybe she can make an exception for Mae? After today, she's the only Original left. That has to count for something."

"If it doesn't, will you tell me when it's going to happen? Give me some warning, so I can—" I broke off, my voice cracking at the thought of having to say goodbye to Mae.

Lev hugged me to his chest, his breath warm against my cheek. "I'll send you a message the second I know anything," he promised. I nodded against him, the fabric of his tunic rubbing my cheek. I pressed myself harder against him, reassured that he'd do whatever he could to help me.

It wasn't until later, as I walked back to my dwelling that I realized even if Lev was able to send a message about Mae, I'd never get it. Not with a broken pulse point.

Lev

A noticeable gloom hung over the gymnasium. No one chatted or exchanged pleasantries. Citizens ran without their usual vigor, still reeling from the news about energy sharing. A few elders had made an appearance, intent on proving they could still produce joules. Their stiff-kneed steps and pained expressions only reinforced the Council's decision.

At the far end of the gymnasium, a young boy celebrated his First Mat Day. Usually a day to celebrate, the people around him gave half-hearted cheers as he completed his first run. It wasn't him I was watching though. It was his second-degree elder. She stood outside of the circle, watching, tears welling in her eyes. It would be the last first run she saw.

I'd spent the morning working up the courage to speak to Tar. It would be a delicate discussion. I couldn't sound too desperate to save Mae, or she'd call me weak. And, if I didn't show enough interest, she'd ignore me. My stomach twisted in knots as I approached the stairs to the underland chambers. These were hidden in the labyrinth of corridors and few Citizens ever made their way down here. Dank and cool, the air smelled different. Rows of small holes cut in the ceiling let light from above shine through, but there were no windows, no connection with the outside at all.

The Scientists had built the underland first as an underground bunker. I didn't know how far the chambers extended under the surface, no Citizen did.

Tar sat at her station, a hologram projected in front of her. With access to innumerable applications other Citizens never knew about, she and the other Council members could have run the City without ever leaving the underland. "Lev," she said, "I wasn't expecting you." I listened for annoyance, but there was none. She sounded happy to see me. I wondered what I could have done right to get that reaction.

I took a deep breath. "I came to talk to you about something. I need a favour."

She gave a disgruntled sigh. "Overseers don't ask for favours. Especially from a Councillor."

My rehearsed speech froze in my throat.

She gave a harsh laugh. "I can see from the look on your face that wasn't the answer you wanted."

I gritted my teeth. With a curt nod of my head, I turned on my heel, ready to leave.

"Don't run off so fast," she said, her tone conciliatory. "There's something I wanted to talk to you about." I hesitated. I'd come to save Mae, and if I left, I had no chance of success. I knew how Tar worked, I'd seen the bargains she made. So, I took a deep breath and faced her.

Her eyebrows rose slightly, expectantly. "I put your name in for a match."

"What?" I stared at her in disbelief. "You can't do that!"

"I can and did. You were dragging your feet, probably waiting for that female, Kaia, to put her name in. Which is ridiculous because you'd never match with her."

My cheeks flushed red.

She sat back with a satisfied grin and with a few swishes of her finger, a row of female Citizens' profiles floated in front of me.

The third from the left was Sari. I widened my eyes in surprise. Match with Sari? Kaia's best friend? Tar saw my eyes linger on her and pounced. "Good genetics, not as high on intelligence as I would have liked, but she has overseers on both sides and one Council Member from the first generation."

"You can't force me to make a match."

"Can't I?"

My face flushed and I fought to stay calm. This was typical Tar, a manipulation game to get what she wanted. There had to be a way to use this to my advantage. My mind clicked through possibilities. "The female has to agree to the match."

"Yes, and why wouldn't she? Your genetics are excellent."

"She wouldn't want me if I was unfit to be an overseer."

Tar narrowed her eyes at me. It was a dangerous bargaining chip, but it was all I had.

"Females might think the whispers about the mark on my face are true. Maybe there are more genetic defects than you'll admit. Especially if I became an embarrassment to you. A failure as an overseer."

Tar glared. "You're self-destructive. I'm trying to help you, give you a future in the City."

"You're not helping me," I snorted. "You're controlling me."

Tar hooted with laughter. "You think I'll stand by and let you match with Kaia? Is that what the two of you were plotting last night in the orchard?" Colour drained from my face. Tar stood up and took a step toward me, intimidating even though I was a head taller. "You think I don't know?" I shut my eyes, turning away from her. When she spoke, a fine spray of spit hit my cheek. "If you saw Kaia's profile you'd realize, she'll never match."

I curled my fingers into fists as anger boiled through me. "You're just saying that because she matters more to me than you do." Even as the words left my lips, I knew they would incite her. Maybe I *was* self-destructive.

Her hand came up fast and the slap caught me off guard. I reeled, dizzy.

"How dare you," she hissed at me. "After all I've done for you!"

Her loss of composure gave me a small victory. I'd touched a nerve. "What you've done has been for you. You've never asked me what I want." I put my finger to the corner of my mouth, wiping away a trickle of blood.

"And what *do* you want?" Her voice dripped with derision.

"Reinstate energy sharing. Do that and I'll agree to match."

"Energy sharing?" she repeated. "Why? So the female can save her elder for what? A few more weeks? A month?"

Determined not to let her distract me or talk me out of it, I stood my ground, meeting her dark, flinty eyes. My promise to Kaia within reach.

She stared at me as if I was a stranger. "You're willing to bargain for *her?*"

Again, I nodded.

Clamping my lips shut against her taunts, I didn't flinch. For once, I had the upper hand.

"My choice for your match," she whispered, slowly, "is Sari." Her face lit up as mine paled.

A row of potential matches and she'd picked the one that would most wound Kaia. Anger burned in my chest and I threw her a hateful look. Never had I despised Tar more than this moment.

She gave me a slippery, triumphant smile. "You agree?" she asked and waited for me to give her a stiff nod. "I'll have the energy-sharing rule reversed and the elders can rest easy."

I'd done it. Whatever else I'd agreed to, at least Mae had been saved. As I turned to go, Tar's voice punctured the air. "One more thing, Lev."

I looked at Tar. A smug expression slithered across her face. "The next time you try to bargain with me, check your facts. The order to take Kaia's elder was given this morning."

A strangled scream of frustration lodged itself in my throat. I tore down the corridor and up the stairs desperate to find Kaia. When I got to the walkway, I barrelled into Citizens, too panicked to stop and send her a message.

"Lev!" Across the stream someone called my name. I turned and caught a flash of Sari's golden hair, her arm raised in a wave. "Send Kaia a message," I shouted. "They're coming for Mae!" Or had they already?

Sari shouted something after me, but I was running too fast to hear her. *Please, don't let it be too late.* The words repeated in my head until I was at Kaia's dwelling. My breath rasped in my throat as I lifted my fist to hammer on her door. *Please, don't let it be too late.*

Kaia

"Mae?" I called when I came home from work. Sy sat on the balcony, staring at the Mountain. *In one of his moods,* I thought, with a resigned sigh.

He turned around and looked at me with red-rimmed eyes. "She's gone, Kaia. They took her this morning."

I stared at him, numb with disbelief. "No," I muttered and shook my head. "No."

Sy stood up and took a few steps towards me. Frown lines were etched deep into his cheeks.

I never got to say goodbye. I always thought we'd know when her time was up. That we'd be warned.

Lev had promised to tell me.

Had he tried? I stared at my finger: 125 glowed, peaceful, ever present.

I felt it then, a collapse in my chest, like the ground was giving way. My knees buckled and Sy swooped in and scooped me up like I was a child.

"Mae!" I cried, rocking against him. "Mae!" My sobs echoed in the dwelling and my throat ached.

Mae was gone.

I wept, soaking Sy's tunic with my tears. "You need to sleep," Sy said, leading me to my capsule. But that wasn't what I needed. I needed Mae.

I refused to leave my capsule the next day and the one after that. Grief made me ache. It hurt to breathe, a throbbing hollowness made every muscle sore.

Sy tried talking to me, telling me that Lev had come, bringing food and apologies. He wanted to see me, but I kept the door on my capsule locked. I didn't want to see anyone. Not Lev, not Sari and not Sy.

I lay in my capsule for days, but still my pulse point glowed 125.

I stared at the number like it was a cruel joke. The malfunctioning pulse point that allowed me to retreat from life had also kept me from Mae when she needed me the most.

My need for the toilet was the only thing that pulled me from the capsule. Sy ambushed me on one of my trips back to the safety of my dark cocoon. "Kaia, you have to eat," Sy begged.

"No." After not talking for so long, the words came out in a croak.

"At least come to the balcony. There's a harvest moon tonight. It's rare. Something to see."

I ignored him and crawled back inside, pulling the capsule door shut behind me. I held up my finger, the hologram projecting against the white wall of the capsule and opened the first memory I'd ever saved. It was Mae, younger, her hair still dark, skin smoother on her cheeks, eyes bright. She was on a bridge, the orchard in the background, giving me my first lesson in saving a memory. "That's right, now close your eyes and relive it. Your memory chip will capture it and store it for you." Darkness followed and then the loop repeated.

I fell asleep listening to her voice.

When morning came, I could hear Sy tending to his plants, moving back and forth with baskets of harvested vegetables from the balcony. I stuck a hesitant foot out of the capsule, shivering at the change in temperature from the warm, stale air inside.

Sy's face brightened when I joined him on the balcony. "You're up," he said. A lemon, its rind garish against the pallor of his skin and tunic, made me wince. I thought he'd be lost to me, spiralling deeper into Mae's death, too far to find his way out. Instead, he looked at me, eyes set with determination.

"I'm hungry."

"Good. There's lots to eat. I thought I might take some vegetables to the market today, we have so much extra." He caught himself too late. There was one less mouth to feed. The unintended cruelty of his words knocked the wind out of me.

And then, his eyes lighted on my finger. Still glowing with 125. "You went to the gymnasium?" he asked.

"It's broken. Has been for days."

"Broken," he frowned, "Are you getting messages? Is the tracking working?"

I shook my head. I'd become invisible. Any other Citizen who didn't show up at work or produce joules would have drawn the attention of the overseers. But my broken pulse point had allowed me the luxury of grieving for three days. As if on cue, a hammering at the door jolted me. I looked at Sy. "Overseers?" I whispered. I knew they'd come eventually and threaten me with punishment if I didn't return to work.

"I'll get it." Sy straightened his tunic, handed me the lemon and went to the door. I heard muffled voices and then Lev appeared.

We stared at each other. Something about him was different, or maybe it was me. I had changed. Where was the usual spark I felt when I saw him? Losing Mae had turned me into a paler version of myself. I dug my nails into the lemon, the rind pressing uncomfortably against the flesh of my finger, the sharp, citrus odour filling the air.

Sy retreated to the kitchen. I turned my back to Lev and stared across the City, blinking back tears.

Lev moved behind me and a sudden need for comfort made me want to collapse against him. I took a shaky breath. Sadness swelled in my chest, stretching my ribs to the point of bursting.

But he stayed an arm's length away. A confusing, unspeakable distance between us. "I saw you from the walkway," he said apologetically. "I thought maybe you were ready to see me." But I wasn't. One look at my face and he knew that. "Kaia?" He asked, tenuous. "By the time I found out, she had already been taken." His voice cracked with emotion. "I'm so sorry." I expected him to reach out for me, even with Sy in the other room, but he stayed where he was. I turned to look at him. "Have you read our other messages?" A flash of guilt crossed his face.

"I haven't checked." But even if I tried, they wouldn't be there.

"I'm sorry," he said again, his eyes searching my face.

I didn't like the way he looked at me. Apologetic and guilty. It made anger well up in me. I turned away again. "Everything's changed," I whispered.

"What do you mean?" He came to stand beside me and we both stared out over the City.

"Was it like this when Kellan died?"

His Adam's apple bobbed when he swallowed. Lev wrinkled his brow, trying to remember. "I don't know. I was only four." His fingers grazed mine.

A sob escaped my lips, and in an instant, Lev pulled me to him, wrapping his arms around me. "I'm so sorry," he whispered. "So sorry." I wanted to melt there, let my bones liquefy and seep into him so I had the strength to go on. I couldn't do it on my own. It hurt too much.

We didn't hear anyone approach until a throat was cleared, a signal that we weren't alone. Wiping my eyes, I turned. Sari stood in the dwelling, staring at us. I almost didn't recognize her. She'd cut her hair. Short at the back but longer on top, it fell in a swoop across her forehead. A strange look crossed her face and Lev backed away from me.

"You said you'd send me a message if she was ready for visitors," she said, an accusatory note in her voice.

"I just got here," Lev mumbled.

A frown creased her forehead. She shot him a glance and turned to me. "Kaia, I'm sorry," she said, but moved closer to Lev. They stood shoulder to shoulder, united in their concern for me. "I've been covering for you at the clinic, but the supervisors are starting to wonder."

I nodded, grateful. I'd have to find my way back to normalcy soon. Like every other Citizen who resumed their daily life. *But this can't be like every other Citizen. Who else has ever hurt this much?*

"We have lots to tell you." It was her 'we' that didn't sit right. A subtle intonation as she said the word, almost triumphant.

Lev shook his head at her. "Sari, I don't think now—"

"Your hair," I sighed. Sari's hand went to the back of her head, stroking the curve of her skull.

"I had it cut yesterday. I'm still getting used to it." But she held her head high. There was no shame in its length. She hadn't been forced to shear it before she'd found a mate.

"Who is he?" I asked, relieved to have some good news to focus on. The two of them stared at me. The pause grew long and awkward. "What?" I asked. "Who is it?"

Finally, Lev cleared his throat. "Me. She matched with me."

I saw the guilty flush rise up her neck. Her eyes skittered across my face.

I stared at Lev. He stepped away from Sari. "This isn't how I wanted you to find out."

"Matched?" I sputtered.

"It was out of our control," Sari's voice was shrill, pleading that I listen. "I couldn't say no. When the matchmaker came, he said the Council had already approved it."

I took a shaky breath and clung to the railing. Shock or days without eating made my knees weak. I sank to the balcony floor. Sari's voice became like static. Her hand was on my shoulder. I swatted at her, twisting away from her touch.

"You should have waited to tell her," Lev muttered angrily.

"I didn't want her to find out from someone else," she replied and turned back to me. "I promise, Kaia, I didn't ask to match with him. The matchmaker practically *commanded* it. I had no choice."

I knew how desperately Sari wanted status. A match with an overseer would elevate her profile in the City. But did it have to be with Lev?

She knew the feelings we had for each other. Couldn't she have said no and spared me? Or was she so status-hungry that matching with Lev was worth risking our friendship?

And Lev. There were no excuses for what he'd done. He'd abandoned me when I needed him most.

I shut my eyes and sat there, unmoving. Mae had told me about statues. Stones that were carved to look like people. That was how I felt: cold, hard and frozen in time. Sari fluttered around me, still trying to explain, but I ignored her. "We should go," Lev said to Sari. His words lingered in my mind. I wanted to go too. But where? There was no escape in the City. I was trapped.

As they backed away from the balcony, they promised to come back and check on me. "Send me a message if you need anything," Sari said. I could hear the anguish in her voice, but she didn't know how it felt. She'd never had feelings for anyone like I had for Lev. She'd never understand how deeply her betrayal had cut me.

But Lev *did* know and his muttered apologies turned my stomach.

I shut my eyes and receded into a deep, dark pit of grief.

Lev

I tried to block the image of Kaia on the balcony. I should have been honest and told her what had happened: that I'd bargained with Tar and lost.

That I'd failed.

I plodded along the walkway, lost in my thoughts, barely aware that Sari was beside me. "You're right," she finally admitted. "We shouldn't have told her." Her voice caught. "I knew it would be hard for her, but I thought the sooner she knew," her voice trailed off.

"She's still dealing with Mae's balancing."

"She must feel so alone," Sari whispered and then stopped walking. "What have we done?" she moaned. Tears welled in her eyes.

I had no answer for her.

"It wasn't just the matchmaker who came to me, you know. Tar was there too."

Of course she was.

"I said no at first, but she refused to listen. She was determined that I match with you. She said she'd chosen me specially." Sari looked at me as if I had answers for her. "I was worried about what would happen if I said no."

I felt a stab of guilt on two fronts. Not only had I betrayed Kaia, but now Sari had been pulled into Tar's plot.

"I was so excited to be matched," Sari's voice quivered and she swallowed back a sob.

Usually a celebration, Tar's manipulations had ruined an

event most Citizens looked forward to. "You don't deserve this," I told her.

A lock of blond hair fell over her face. She didn't move it away, instead she blinked at me from underneath it. "I keep hoping that if Kaia gets used to the idea, she'll see it's not so bad. Her two best friends will be together. It's kind of perfect in a way."

"Maybe," I sighed, but it would be a long time before I forgot the image of Kaia, huddled on the balcony, broken and abandoned.

A group of Citizens walked by, eyeing the two of us. Word about the match might have spread. Sari cleared her throat and brushed her hair into place. "Are you going back to the gymnasium?" she asked. My midday break was almost over.

"Yes." We stood on the walkway, both of us suddenly awkward. Was she waiting for me to ask to see her later, or join her for an evening meal, as other couples would? I couldn't bring myself to do it.

"I should get back to work too," Sari sighed. "See you later then."

I watched her go, the pang of guilt growing sharper. I'd never be the match Sari deserved when Kaia was the only one I thought about. Let Tar do her worst to me, I thought with fiery conviction. No punishment could be harsher than what I'd just done to Kaia.

My pace quickened with urgency as I made my way to the gymnasium. Had it really only been a few days ago that Kaia and I had sat under the tree after the energy-sharing rule had been revoked? It felt like years ago. Stopping in the middle of the walkway, I sent Kaia a message. *I'll be in the orchard. There are things I couldn't say before. Things you need to know. Please come.*

People moved past me as I waited for Kaia's reply, but none came. It didn't matter. I'd go to the orchard after my shift and wait for her all night if I had to. When she got there, I'd tell her the truth about what Tar had done. We'd make a plan and together, we'd fight for what we wanted.

Kaia

Thoughts of Mae, Sari and Lev made sleep impossible. After hiding in my capsule for so long, I needed space, room to breathe and think, so I made my way to the balcony. This late at night, the City was dark and silent except for the hum of the huge contraption that purified our air.

An overseer approached on the walkway below. I backed away from the railing and held my breath, waiting for a knock on the door. But none came and a few moments later, I saw her crossing a bridge to the other side of the City.

125 glowed under my skin, still undetected. I should confess. It was wrong to keep it a secret, I was stealing from the City.

A painful lump formed in my throat at what the City had stolen from me. Mae had been dragged away. And now Sari and Lev were matched. My fears were coming true. I would be left with no one.

I didn't hear Sy approach. His voice startled me. "You should be sleeping."

I shook my head and didn't turn around. I could feel him hovering.

"Kaia," he began, his words stilted, "She knew they were coming." He moved closer, tentative. "She lived a good, long life."

The more he struggled to talk to me, the more alone I felt. I wanted to know that she'd had a final message for me, that she'd forgiven me for not doing more to save her, for not being here to say goodbye.

"Balancing is a given. It will happen to all of us," Sy said. "You have to move on."

I pulled my gaze away from the City and turned to him. "You never did." Hurt made the words sharper than I meant them to be.

He sighed. "It was different with Raina." A dim light from inside our dwelling illuminated the sharp angles of his face.

"How?" I muttered. My whole life he'd been removed from me, darting into faraway recesses of his mind where I couldn't reach him. But I'd always had Mae.

He took a deep breath and spoke before he exhaled. "Raina didn't die, Kaia. She left."

I looked at him with disbelief.

"She went to the Mountain."

I gave a mirthless laugh at the preposterousness of what he was saying. "You're making it up," I shook my head at him, wondering why he'd try to trick me at a time like this.

"I wish I was." He stared in the direction of the Mountain, but it wasn't with the usual forlorn expression. Sy puckered his mouth, as if he was trying to regain control and put the memory in order. "I've been carrying this secret with me, waiting, wondering when to tell you. *If* I should tell you." A pained look crossed his face. "You need to know the truth."

"Which is what?"

"After you were born, we made the decision to leave. We didn't want our lives shadowed by balancings and overseers." He held up his finger, "Or to be ruled by this." Forty-five glowed through his skin. Instinctively, I felt for the raised bump on my finger. Its beat remained still, like a dead thing under my skin.

"Raina was convinced that if we got to the Mountain, the Prims would help us. They weren't what the City had led us to believe. We made a plan and left in the night. I carried you in my arms. This tiny, perfect package," his voice softened.

He paused and I leaned in, addled by doubt. The story was incredible. Citizens didn't leave the City. The dangers outside were too great: the storms, the scorching sun that could fry the skin off our bodies in minutes, Prims, the beasts that Mae had sworn existed. I eyed him suspiciously. "How were you going to get out?"

"Tunnels. The Scientists dug them when the City was being built. She knew the way, one of the secrets she'd learned in the underland."

I frowned trying to make sense of the story

"Raina went into the tunnel first, I followed. But, I didn't have her blind faith that we'd survive out there. I-I," he stumbled, emotion choking his words. "At the last minute, I couldn't do it."

"You let her go on her own?"

Sy didn't answer.

"You let her go outside? On her own?" I asked again, fury replacing the shock.

"We were supposed to protect you. How could we, out there?" he broke off, his voice trailing to nowhere. "What if something happened to us? What if you were left alone? In the end, I let her go. Told her to run, that she had a better chance of surviving if I stayed behind and covered for her. I promised her I'd follow with you." He shook his head, sagging with the weight of the memory.

"But you never did."

He shook his head.

Breath rattled through me. The way he stared at the Mountain, lost, he was staring after Raina, at the life they could have had. The life he'd let slip away from him. From me.

"Did Mae know?"

Sy gave a slow nod of his head.

My head pounded. Mae had known and kept it a secret from me.

Sy moved in close and grabbed my shoulders, forcing me to face him. His breath was hot in my face and his eyes bright. "We can find her, Kaia. Together."

"Find her? After all these years?" I stared at him. Grief had addled his brain. His tenuous grip on reality had slipped from his fingers. I measured my words carefully. "She's not still out there. No one could survive outside."

He narrowed his eyes at me and tightened his grip on my shoulders. "That's what they want us to believe."

"What do you mean?"

"Raina thought, she was sure, that outside wasn't as dangerous as the Council told us. They want us to be afraid so they can control us."

"The City protects us—" I started, but even as I said the words, I knew they weren't true. I'd said as much to Lev in the orchard.

"All these years, I made excuses to stay. First, you were too young, then I wanted to stay for Mae. But now," he broke off. "It's time, Kaia. We can go to her, find the life you were meant to have." Sy gripped my shoulders. "Think about it, The Prims aren't hammering on the dome, trying to get in. Not anymore."

"They could all be dead," I said, pushing his hands off my shoulders. "Did you think of that?"

Sy shook his head. "They were alive when Raina left."

"How do you know all this?"

"I told you, Raina knew things."

I tried a different tactic. "What about the garden? My work at the clinic? Lev? Sari?" Even as I said the words, I knew another Citizen would be reassigned to our jobs in a heartbeat. And Lev and Sari weren't a reason to stay. They were a reason to leave.

"It's time, Kaia. I'm all out of excuses. You know as well as I do what your future in the City will be."

Could I do it? Leave? Risk my life on Sy's promises?

"If we're going to go, it has to be soon, before anyone discovers your broken pulse point." Sy's eyes were bright and excited. "What do you say?"

I looked out over the City. The sun was rising and a warm light filled the dome. There'd be no security out there. No dome to protect me from outside.

But I didn't have security inside either.

I turned to Sy and took a deep breath. "When do we leave?"

Lev

Every minute I didn't think about Kaia was an achievement. She preyed on my mind constantly, especially during the mind-numbing shifts at the gymnasium. Staring out over the running mats, I couldn't stop myself from thinking about her. Why hadn't she responded to my messages? I'd gone to the orchard last night and sat for hours, but she never came. If she'd just answer my messages, or agree to meet with me, I could explain that I'd tried to beat Tar at her own game and lost.

"Lev, you're requested in MM 359," an overseer said, inter-rupting my thoughts. She slid into my spot at the railing.

"By who?"

She shrugged, her eyes already glazing over as she stared down at the gymnasium floor.

MM 359 was a matchmaker's room. I'd gone there this morn-ing to explain my plight and ask them to reconsider the match with Sari. The matchmaker had listened but shaken his head at my request. "The Council has already approved the match," he'd said. "My hands are tied."

What if Sari had also asked for the match to be undone? Maybe she'd realized it was a mistake to betray Kaia. Was she willing to risk Tar's threats for her friend? I walked there as quickly as I could, my mind spinning with possibilities.

When I opened the door to MM 359, I saw Sari. She was talk-ing to the matchmaker and for a second I felt a rush of optimism.

But then I noticed Tar. One look at the smug expression on her face and I knew my hopes for a different outcome had been foolish.

"Welcome to your matching ceremony, Lev." I gritted my teeth at Tar's words. "A dwelling has been secured for you and your mate," she glanced at Sari. "There's no reason to delay." Some newly matched couples had to wait months until a dwelling was made available. Trust Tar to use her influence to make sure I jumped to the top of the list.

"This is happening so fast. I'm barely used to the idea that I'm matched." Sari's eyes flitted warily between me and Tar.

All the reasons against the match rose in my throat, but was there any point? No doubt Tar had a backup plan. I'd tried to outwit her before and failed. If I backed out now, what would Tar do? Find a reason to balance Kaia? Punish me in a way worse than this? Instead, I gave Sari a thin-lipped smile. "No reason to wait," I said, echoing Tar.

Sari blinked at me. There was so much still unsaid between us. Tar cleared her throat, a signal to the matchmaker that he should begin. The formal matching was quick, just a matter of linking our pulse points with a Councillor—in this case, Tar—present to approve the match.

"Raise your forefingers," the matchmaker commanded.

I hesitated.

"Lev," Tar's voice was a warning. Reluctantly, I raised my finger.

Sari gave me a nervous smile as our fingertips touched. There was a faint tremor as the pulse points connected. "You are matched," the matchmaker said and smiled at both of us. One corner of Tar's mouth went up in a satisfied smirk.

"What a perfect couple," Tar said proudly. "You'll be the envy of your cohorts," I cringed at Tar's words. In her mind, Sari was a mate befitting a future leader.

I swallowed back a lump and grit my teeth. "I should get back to work."

Sari bit her lip and nodded.

The matchmaker looked surprised. "Most new mates go for a walk to celebrate. Maybe to the orchard or along the stream?" he suggested.

I gave him a cool look. The last thing I wanted was to be paraded through the City as proof that Tar had won. I opened my mouth to argue and caught the look that Tar shot Sari. Before I could say anything, Sari said, "That's a good idea. I'm sure Tar can explain to your supervisor why you'll be late for work."

I gaped at her. Our match was no cause for celebration. Sari cast a quick glance at Tar, who nodded approvingly.

I stiffened. So, Tar had found a way to get to Sari. Had it been bribes or more threats? It didn't matter. This match was a sham and Sari knew it as well as I did. As soon as I talked to Kaia, I'd come back to the matchmaker and explain how Tar had orchestrated the match under false pretenses. I'd push for the match to be dissolved. Sari would be embarrassed, but I'd argue that she deserved a mate who wanted to be with her. Not someone who would forever be pining for someone else.

Sari lifted her pulse point and her hologram floated in the air between us. "Look! There you are!" My face showed up as one of the icons, and I was on her locator map as well. "Should we meet up later? To make our dinner? You can join me in my dwelling until we move into our own."

Her words were for Tar's benefit, not mine. I was sure of it. I ignored her offer. "I should get back to the gymnasium. I don't want people thinking I get special treatment because of who my elder is."

"I guess I should go back to work too," Sari sighed. "We're short-staffed at the clinic."

Her words hung between us, taking up more space than the four people in the room. I gave Tar a quick bow, silently cursing her, and nodded to the matchmaker. I held the door open for Sari, but Tar called her back. "A word, Sari?" The expression on Sari's face hardened, but she obeyed. What choice did she have?

As I went back to the gymnasium, I composed a message to Kaia. As long as we stayed in the City, we could never be free. Not from Tar, or the whims of the Council. Maybe leaving the City was our only option. Could we do it? I looked out the Dome, at the barren, cracked plain that separated us from the Mountain. The question haunted me as I stood on the balcony. Was it possible to survive out there?

Kaia

"We'll go the way Raina did," Sy said. "Through the underland." "The underland?" I repeated. I'd never been down there, few Citizens had. Its mystery was part of City lore. If a child was caught misbehaving, elders threatened to send them to the underland.

"Do you know how she found it?"

"The way out?"

I nodded.

He gave me a bleak look. "She said it was better if I didn't know."

I frowned at him. Doubts swirled.

But Sy forged on, his mind locked on one target: escape. "The tunnel will take us to the windfarm. We'll go just before dawn. Once we're outside, we stay beside the stream and go to the Mountain."

At his usual time, he left to work in the garden, swearing he was clear-headed even though we'd been up all night. He left me with a list of things to prepare while he was gone. I tried to rest, knowing we had a long night ahead of us, but my mind was spinning.

When Sy came home loaded with supplies, his eyes shone bright and he spoke in rapid bursts. His manic behaviour made me anxious. Could I trust him? After all these years of worrying about his mental fitness, I was willing to follow him outside. A saner me would have thought *I* was the crazy one. Maybe Sy's madness infected me too? Is this what grief did?

I stood mute as Sy packed our satchels, stuffed them with things he'd collected from the garden and our dwelling: a drinking gourd, one of the emergency ones every dwelling had in case our water purification system went down. It had a spout that Sy said could clean 1,000 gallons of water. He warned me the water outside might not be safe to drink. He also packed a pot, wrapped in an extra tunic; a pair of his bamboo gardening shoes, the dried mud scraped onto the floor and left in a dusty pile; a clean bedroll bound tightly with twine. "This," Sy said, "you need to keep handy at all times. It is the most important tool or weapon you'll have with you." It was Mae's knife, the one she always used to prepare dinner. How many times had I watched her chop vegetables with it, the metal blade slicing through beets and avocado, dicing carrots? Swallowing back the wave of grief that threatened to sweep me up, I let him attach it to a belt around my waist.

Sy held up thick, rubbery leaves newly harvested from the garden. "Aloe," he said squeezing the leaf so clear goo oozed out. "The sun can burn. This will help. And garlic." He held up the bulbs still wrapped in papery skin. "Rubbing it on your skin will deter insects. We have to eat as much of it as we can. It will make our blood unappealing."

I grabbed his arm. "Our blood?"

"There are insects that suck blood outside. Don't worry, they're small."

He gave me a look of determination. "I knew one day, we'd join her, Kaia."

I gave him the bravest smile I could and looked around our dwelling. Bereft of us, the space was just that: a space. Sy's garden on the balcony would wither and die without him to tend it. Mae's half-finished mending still sat where she'd left it. Impulsively, I grabbed a scrap of fabric she'd been using and brought it to my face. Her smell lingered on it. I held it in my hand, squeezing it in my fist.

Lev

"What are you doing here?" Sari's voice made me jump. I hadn't heard her coming. I'd ignored her messages and had been waiting in the orchard since my shift at the gymnasium had ended.

Of course, now that we were matched, she could find me wherever I was. Tar didn't have to keep track of me anymore, not when she had Sari. "I was supposed to meet someone," I replied. The sky outside had turned dark. I'd spent another night waiting for nothing.

"Kaia?" Sari asked.

I looked at her and saw the worry on her face.

"Yes."

Sari sat on the ground beside me, gracefully bending her slender legs to one side. "I've been covering for her at the clinic. I told them she'd been quarantined with a virus. But it's been days. They're starting to wonder." Sari's lie had bought Kaia more time off than most people had in their lives. "She has to leave her dwelling soon, don't you think?"

"She hasn't responded to any of my messages."

Sari hesitated and looked like she had something to say, then decided against it. "Do you think she'll forgive us?"

"You maybe. But it's because of me that Mae's gone and we're—"

"Matched," Sari finished. "I keep wondering if it's better this way. Her two best friends, together."

"Sari—" I held up my hand. I didn't want to listen to her justifications. All they did was grate on my nerves.

Sari rose on her knees and leaned towards me. Before I could stop her, she put her lips on mine, pressing herself against me. If I closed my eyes, the taste of her was familiar enough that I could pretend it was Kaia. I didn't push her away. I should have, but I didn't. Missing Kaia, guilt and regret, all the things I'd been feeling disappeared as Sari's mouth moved against mine.

She pulled away first, smiling.

I gulped. A hot flush spread up my neck. What if Kaia had come and seen us? Sari was sitting so close that when I jumped up, she fell backwards. "I have to go!" I said.

Hurt and anger flashed across Sari's face as she stood up. "Where? To find her? What's the point? You'll never match with her! You're the son of a Councillor! She's nothing."

I turned on Sari. "She's not nothing!"

"She is in the City. Councillor Tar explained things to me, Lev. You need to think about the future. *Our* future."

"She bribed you, didn't she? Promised you things to match with me."

Sari met my eyes with a steely look of determination. "We could be happy if you'd give it a chance."

I looked at her with disgust, then turned and ran.

Kaia

Night had settled again on the City. We'd been sitting in the darkness for hours.

"Kaia!" Lev's cries broke the silence. "Kaia!" He pounded on the door.

I looked at Sy, who shook his head and held a finger to his lips.

"Kaia, please! Open the door! I need to talk to you!" Hearing his voice made me wince.

I squeezed my eyes shut and covered my ears. I wouldn't get to say goodbye to him, or feel his arms around me one last time. But no matter how hard I pressed on my ears, I could still hear him. "It's not what you think," Lev shouted through the door.

"Be quiet!" a neighbour yelled. "Or I'll get an overseer!"

Tears prickled in my eyes. *Just go, Lev*, I silently begged. *Don't make this harder for me than it already is.*

"Kaia, please open the door!" He was angry. I covered my mouth to stifle my own cries. "Just. Open. The. Door." Each word was punctuated with a slap on the door. He'd probably sent me messages that had gone unanswered. It was better this way. The less he knew the better.

"What are you doing? Get moving. You don't live there!" another neighbour shouted.

Lev's voice changed from tearful to resolute. "Tomorrow, Kaia. I'll be waiting for you in the orchard tomorrow night. And the day after that and the day after that. I'll wait as long as I have to until you're ready to talk to me."

Oh Lev. Tears trickled down my cheeks and it took everything I had to stay crouched on the floor and let him walk away. For the rest of the night, I wondered if I'd made the right choice.

And finally, it was time. The door shut after us as we walked down the stairs with our bags. Solar-powered lights along the walkway glowed so we clung to the shadows. We saw no other Citizens. Except for the hum of the air purifier, the City was silent. My stomach churned at the thought of what we were about to do.

We walked towards the gymnasium. There were always over-seers stationed here; the gymnasium was open all hours. The sound of a lone runner greeted us as we drew closer. Sy's pace slowed. I hung back, nervous. We hadn't done anything wrong, not yet. Or was conspiring to escape a punishable offence?

A young overseer, a female I knew, stood at the entrance. Sy raised a hand in greeting. She furrowed her brow, taking in our bulging satchels. "I'm Sy. I work in the garden. I forgot to bring these to the storeroom yesterday," Sy explained, gesturing at our bags, his voice friendly. "New potatoes." The female gave us quizzical looks. I offered a friendly smile, even though my mouth quivered with nerves. "Mind if we go this way?" Sy said.

Were there storerooms in the underland? I didn't know and neither did the female. She hesitated.

Sy reached into his satchel and pulled out a white-fleshed potato. Dirt still clung to its skin. He tossed it to the female. She caught it, and in a flash, it disappeared under her tunic. She turned away, her gaze once more on the Citizen inside the gym-nasium. I ducked behind Sy as we quickly shuffled towards the stairs that led into the underland.

As the stairwell spiralled down into complete darkness, my steps grew more apprehensive. Curling my feet around the edge of each stair, I pressed my palm flat against the wall, steadying myself. Dizzy and disoriented, I breathed a sigh of relief when we reached the bottom. The air felt different in the underland: cool and musty.

The corridor that stretched before us was deserted and, except for small, square openings in the ceiling, dark. Sy held up his finger and his pulse point's hologram wavered in front of us. He swiped across the memory icon and selected the image of Mountain and instantly one of his memories appeared. The same corridor captured sixteen years earlier when he and Raina had walked through it. His memory, saved from that night, became our map for escape.

We felt our way along the wall following the memory. There were doors every few metres. A few were marked with signs like "Surgery," "Storage," or "Councillor Chambers." I caught whiffs of antiseptic. Familiar in the clinic, the scent clashed with the moist air of the underland. Behind one door came deep male voices. My heart thumped in my chest and I tripped over my feet, stifling a gasp with my hand. Sy put a reassuring hand on my arm, steadying me.

We kept walking further down the dark corridor. The ground grew uneven. In front of me, the hallway stretched forever in the gloom and was lined with endless doors. What was behind all of them? More storage? I wondered how far the underland extended. Was the maze of secret corridors as big as the City?

Sy's memory showed that we had to turn down a smaller hallway. I looked around, feeling the cool clay walls. There was no corner, no hallway branching off this one. Sy reached out, patting the walls, the hologram momentarily disappearing. From somewhere deeper in the underland, a cough and a moan.

"Sy," I said in barely a whisper. I tugged on his sleeve to turn back. He shook his head, patting the walls more frantically. It was useless. Whatever escape route he and Raina had found before had been sealed off.

The cough came again. I started at the familiarity of it, as if Mae's voice was haunting me. I wanted to get out of this place. And then, a triumphant fist clench from Sy. He grabbed my hand and jammed my fingers between a crack in the clay wall. "Here!"

He pressed his shoulder against the concealed door and it opened into a tunnel. I squinted into the darkness. Sy stooped, ducking his head. The tunnel was half as high as the corridor and just wide enough to accommodate his shoulders. When he slid the door back into place, we were immersed in complete, suffocating darkness. I gulped. I didn't know what existed at the end of the tunnel.

Sy held up his finger and the hologram reappeared. It was no help to us now. The memory was also pitched in blackness, but its faint glimmer of light gave us our bearings. I could hear Sy's breath, heavy and laboured. Fearful.

The tunnel's walls were not adobe. They'd been carved out of the ground with rough tools. We inched through the darkness, worried about tripping over large rocks and uneven terrain. A series of pounding feet through the corridor made us both freeze. Overseers. Sy turned towards the door and bumped into me. We stood in the tunnel, not daring to breathe. Were the overseers coming for us? Had we been discovered?

"Contain them!" a voice ordered. Sy clutched me against him and my bag hung awkwardly off my arm. I thought of the knife. My only weapon. I would run before I would use it. But if I had to, if inflicting harm was my only choice, what then?

"Where do you think you're going?" the same voice, muffled through the adobe walls, asked. I held my breath, waiting for the door to be pushed open.

There was a scuffle in the corridor, a child's scream and then a thump against the wall. Silence.

"Jacob," the voice, clearly an overseer's, growled. "What is she doing here?"

The voice that answered trembled with fury. "You hit a ten-year-old!"

"Doesn't matter. Get her out of here."

I went limp with relief. We were still safe. Sy tugged on my sleeve and started walking again. There was no time to waste. The tunnel snaked underground, growing so small that Sy had to crawl on hands and knees to pass through some sections. Dust-filled air made it hard to breathe. What if there was no end to the tunnel? What if it went on forever, winding dark and treacherous underground, a cruel joke by the City to torment would-be escapees?

We'd been in the tunnel for at least half an hour when it finally emptied into a larger space. Sweat dripped down my face and my bag felt like it weighed triple what it had when we left. Though we were still shrouded in darkness, my shoulders didn't rub against the walls. Sy and I could stand beside each other without touching. I set my bag down, stretching my aching back. "I remember this," Sy whispered. He felt along the walls and made a complete circle. "It's the end of the tunnel. Above us is the windfarm."

"How do we get out?" I was desperate for fresh air, even if it meant being outside.

"There was a ladder," he murmured.

I grit my teeth. Nerves left me impatient, my trust for his plan was ebbing away. He strained, reaching for the ceiling, but it was out of his reach. "There is a hatch above us, somewhere. I'll lift you up."

"You don't know where it is?" I looked up, unsure if he could support my weight. My spirits sank. Why had I thought his plan would work? It was ludicrous. Doubt about Sy's mental stability flashed through my mind. What if Raina hadn't escaped? What if she *was* dead and the escape was one of Sy's delusions.

"Kaia!" His voice was sharp. "Give me your hands. You need to get on my shoulders." Sy bent down in front of me. I let him guide me onto his shoulders. Wobbling, I swung one leg over his shoulder, steadied myself and then let the other one follow.

With me holding on to his head for support, Sy stood up carefully. We'd gained the length of my torso and when I reached up, my palms were flat on the ceiling.

Sy took a few steps forward and caught his breath. A rock underfoot made him stumble. I swayed and tried to find my balance, but leaned too far to the right. I was going to fall off! With a startled scream, I banged against the wall, my cheek scraping against the rough stones. Sy's sweaty hands gripped my legs. "Are you okay?" he asked.

"Yeah," I said. My cheek stung, and almost tipping off had done nothing for the lump of fear that was growing in my stomach. I reached out to the wall to begin my search for a trap door that would lead us outside.

Going slowly, I felt hand over hand, trying not to think about how long it would take to cover every centimetre of the chamber. How long did we have until daybreak? An hour? Two?

My hands brushed against something foreign, not the dirt of the walls. Thick wires, the diameter of my finger, ran along the top of the wall. "Wires!" I said excitedly. I followed them with my hands. "Keep going forward."

"Those are from the wind farm!" Sy said. "They'll show us the way outside."

With fumbling fingers, I followed the cords until they curved into the wall and disappeared. I felt all around the wall, but they were gone. Despair started to creep into me.

"There has to be a hatch," Sy whispered, but there was worry in his voice. We'd made it down here unseen, but the City would be waking up soon. If we found a way out after dawn broke, we'd be spotted in the valley. And if we didn't, and Sy's absence at work was noticed...I shuddered at the thought. The overseer who had seen us go into the underland would report it. They'd come looking for us.

And, if we didn't find the hatch, creeping back through the underland was too risky. There was no doubt we'd be discovered. Our presence down here would be treated with suspicion; we'd be questioned. Taking a deep breath, I felt blindly along the wall and the ceiling until, finally, my fingers grazed something that wasn't rock or gravel. "I found it!" A small square door. Pressing my palms on it, I gave it a shove, but it didn't budge. Using all my strength and grunting with effort, I pushed trying to dislodge it. "It's stuck."

"Use your knife," Sy said. Fighting to stay balanced on his shoulders, I reached a hand down to pull the knife from its sheath. As soon as I felt the handle in my palm, I was reminded of Mae. Sy's legs shook with the effort of holding me up. I had to work quickly.

I jabbed the blade into the crevice between the hatch and the ceiling. There was some give, space to wiggle it. But years of no use had cemented the gravel.

Below me, Sy trembled. "Almost," I breathed. I pushed at the door again and this time, grains of sand and grit rained down on our heads.

"Again," Sy coughed.

I hammered on it with my fist, I didn't care anymore about the noise. I needed to be free of the tunnel. And then, an explosion of sand. I turned my head away, choking. Hot, dry air streamed into the tunnel, whipping past my face.

I almost cried with relief at the sight of the sky. I held the knife in my hand and grabbed for the surface. With shaky legs, I stood on Sy's shoulders, hauled myself up, and kicked my legs free. Rolling onto my back, I gulped in air that burned my lungs with its dryness.

I was outside.

I scrambled back to the opening and peered down, looking for Sy. He stood below me, squinting. "Take your bag," he said and tossed it to me. I grabbed a strap and shoved it aside.

"Grab my arm!" I dangled it down in front of him, but he made no move to take it.

"You're not strong enough," he said.

"Yes, I am. Hurry! Before we're spotted!"

He didn't move. "Go, Kaia. I'll cover for you to give you more time. You have to get to the Mountain."

"What?"

"You heard me. Go!"

I stared at him, shocked. "What about you?"

He shook his head. "I'm not going with you. You need to find her, Kaia. You were never mine to keep." He broke off, his voice thick. "Tell her I'm sorry. Tell her I wish I was as brave as she was."

"Sy!" I waved my arm at him. "No! You have to come!" I begged. "I can't do it alone."

"You can. In a few hours, you'll be out of sight of the City, by evening you'll be on the Mountain." He raised his arm, the joules shone through his finger. I reached down and our fingertips touched. "This was always how it was meant to be," he said.

A gust of wind swirled the dust of the valley. I ducked my head under my arm to protect my eyes. When I opened them again and looked into the tunnel, Sy was gone.

"Sy!" I screamed. "Sy! Come back!" I lowered myself down as far as I could without falling in. "Sy!" But I couldn't see anything but dirt walls and Sy's bag, slumped on the ground.

My breath came in hot, hard bursts. He was gone. I raised my head out of the hole and sat on the ground, shock rendering me numb.

"Sy!" Panic came hot and fast on the heels of fear. I was outside. I cowered, pulled my bag to me and crouched low. My heart beat hard in my chest. The City rose in front of me like a beast. In the other direction: the Mountain. Sy had said to find Raina, all we had to do was follow the stream to its source.

But, there was no "we." Sy wasn't coming. I was alone.

And if I dropped back into the tunnel and followed Sy back to our dwelling, what then? My broken pulse point would be discovered. I'd be punished, sent to the underland. I'd have to face Sari and Lev's betrayal.

The sun would be rising soon. As soon as it did, I'd be spotted. With grim understanding, I knew I couldn't stay at the City's walls any longer. I didn't have a choice. I'd left the City.

The door fell too easily into place.

I stared into the vastness that surrounded me. Overwhelmed. Sy had told me the plan. He'd drawn it out for me, insisted that I repeat it to him. Now I knew why.

The stream lay to the east; if I followed it, I'd get to the Mountain. The most direct route took me through the wind farm and past the lightning conductors. Stuffing Mae's knife into my bag, I started walking.

Hundreds of massive windmills stretched across the valley. Their blades cut through the air, collecting energy as the wind propelled them. The whirring was deafening as I trudged towards them. The silvery blades sliced the air like whirling knives. Would they suck me up into the propeller, dice me into a million pieces? As I got closer, the draft grew stronger. I hunched my shoulders, holding my bag against me. Each step required effort, the pull of the air current strong.

I kept going, one foot in front of the other. There was no going back now. It was hard to breathe. The wind got sucked out of my mouth before it even entered my lungs. I struggled, gasping, panic mounting at the force of the blades. Disoriented, I felt myself veer too close to the whizzing metal propellers. I fought against the pull, but the blades dragged me towards them. A scream burst from my mouth. I ducked and fell to my stomach, using my arms to crawl forward. Dust and sand whipped into my eyes, stinging my face. My cries drowned out by the drone of the blades.

Lev

Sy stood in his dwelling doorway, his sunken eyes surveying me. "Where's Kaia?" I asked.

He shifted forward, blocking my entrance. "Not here."

A tremor ran through me. "She has to be. She's not at work. Her locator on my hologram says she's here." When he didn't budge, I tried a different tactic. "She's going to be reported, Sy. I need to see her."

"Reported?"

"She hasn't been to work or the gymnasium in ten days and she isn't responding to messages." I stared at Sy's stooped shoulders and haggard expression. He looked beaten. "Please, tell me where she is?"

"Not here," he whispered.

My chest seized and I pushed past him. "Kaia?" I called. In three strides, I was at her capsule. It lay empty, her blanket neatly folded at the end of the sleeping mat. I stared in shock. I was sure she'd be here.

I turned to Sy. "You must know where she is. If you didn't, you'd be searching for her too." I took a step closer, balling my hands into fists. "Where is she?"

"Gone."

"Where?" I seethed.

"To the Mountain."

He'd lost his mind. The thought rammed itself into my head. I was talking to a crazy person. I pulled up my hologram. Kaia's locator dot blinked in her dwelling. "Did you do something to her?"

"I told you where she is."

I stared at him for a long minute, waiting to see if the tension would make him snap. But, he met my eyes and didn't waver. I left the door open as I exited his dwelling. Kaia was somewhere in the City and I needed to find her.

Raf was already on the balcony at the gymnasium when I arrived for my shift. "You're late," Raf barked. "Where were you?"

"Trying to find someone."

"Who?"

I wasn't in the mood for his questions. "What do you care?" Raf raised an eyebrow at my tone. Below, Citizens pounded on the running mats; their feet collectively made a dull roar.

Raf moved closer. The stubby grey hair of his eyebrows drew together. "I'm your superior. It matters."

If I told him about Kaia, Tar would find out. But she'd find out anyway, eventually. Raf was a senior overseer and knew the City better than anyone. If Sy had done something to Kaia, or Kaia was hiding, Raf could help me find her. And if she had gone to the Mountain as Sy claimed? I shook my head at the impossibility of it. I'd never heard of anyone leaving. "Is it possible for a Citizen to leave?" I asked, lowering my voice.

He hesitated, narrowing his eyes. "Why?"

"Is it?"

"Yes."

I took a deep breath, willing myself to be patient. "How?"

He jerked his head at the dome above the gymnasium. "There's an escape hatch. You've been up there actually. Kellan took you when you were a child." I started at the mention of Kellan's name. "Follow me." He ordered another overseer to cover for us and led me towards a spiral staircase. Off-limits to Citizens, the staircase led to the top of the dome. There was a small landing and below, the whole City stretched out before me. I took in the view, speechless.

He pointed to a coiled rope ladder hanging on the railing. "Escape hatch. See that panel," he pointed to one above our heads. I'd been so distracted by the view, I hadn't noticed the latch or hinges. "It opens up." He jiggled a lock. "No one's used it lately."

I let out a sigh of relief. One problem solved. Kaia hadn't escaped, but that meant Sy had lied to me.

"Has it *ever* been used?" I couldn't imagine climbing down the dome to get to the ground outside.

"Once that I can remember," he said. "It was how Kellan got out the day he—" He left the thought hanging.

Died.

"You don't remember, but he used to bring you up here. I'd come too. We were friends, you know. Trained as overseers together."

Raf held up his finger and swiped open a memory on his holo-gram. Kellan floated in front of me. Angular jaw and cheekbones, brown eyes. In the hologram, their voices echoed off the dome's panels as they climbed the stairs, Kellan held the hand of a child. Me. My legs were barely long enough to climb each step. Kellan smiled down at me and looked up at Raf. "Future overseer," he said pointing at me. The young Raf laughed.

And then, from the top of the lookout, Kellan held me up to survey the City. "Ah! Here it is, Lev! The City!" Raf's memory followed the stream as it meandered past the dwellings, through the garden and orchard.

"I haven't been up here in a long time," Raf said quietly as the hologram disappeared. He turned and looked out over the valley below us. The sun was peeking over the Mountain, casting its warm glow over the dome.

He pointed to a thin tower poking out of the ground like a needle: one of many conductors that dotted the barren valley. The kites attached to them waved in the wind. Meant to goad lightning into striking the metal poles, the kites provided hours of entertainment to children who watched them dip and dive.

"Only Kellan was brave enough to hoist those." The tendons in his face tensed as he clenched his jaw.

What Kellan had done was legendary; it had made him a hero.

A dangerous energy shortage had put the City in jeopardy. The Council came up with a plan to attach the kites to the conductors. But with a storm on the horizon, there wasn't much time. Kellan had volunteered. It was while he was attaching the last kite that he'd fallen to his death with the whole City watching.

"So, why all the questions about escaping?" Raf's permanent frown turned suspicious.

I swallowed. Once I told him what Sy had said, there was no going back. "A female Citizen is missing. Her elder said she escaped. But I think he's lying—"

"Did he say when?" Raf interrupted and gave me a hard look.

"I didn't take him seriously."

Raf moved in so close, I could see faint, grey hairs on his chin, thin and wispy. "Take me to him."

His voice made my skin prickle with fear. With heavy feet, I led him back down the stairs.

From the walkway, I could see Sy on his balcony. Head bowed, hands gripping the railing, a mass of greenery engulfed him. The anger I had melted away. He looked like a sad, broken man up there, waiting for us to come for him.

"Raf, wait. If he's gone crazy, then what? Do we take him away or..." my voice trailed off. Sometimes the hospital could settle Citizens who had temporarily lost touch and other times, they were balanced.

Raf pressed his mouth into a thin line. "You know the answer."

"What if I'm wrong? Maybe I misunderstood."

I wanted to find Kaia, but not like this. She could be hiding within the City. There were lots of places to disappear, especially if she had someone helping her. The real mystery was that her absence had gone undetected, as if she no longer existed.

Raf came down the two steps he'd climbed and stood level with me. "You're an overseer now. We don't make mistakes." He shook his head at me for emphasis. "Come on," he nodded his head. "We'll get to the bottom of this."

I thought of Kaia. I was doing this for her. If Sy knew where she was, if he had done anything to her….Taking a deep breath to steady myself, I raised my hand to knock on the door. No answer. I tried the handle. It wasn't locked.

Sy stayed on the balcony with his back to us when we entered. He didn't even turn around when Raf said, "Sy? We have questions for you." Raf grabbed his wrists, one in each hand and pulled him backwards into the dwelling.

"Where's the female?" Raf looked at me for her name.

"Kaia," I supplied, my voice hoarse.

"Gone."

"Gone where?" Raf tightened his grip and Sy winced.

"To the Mountain."

"How?"

"It doesn't matter. You're too late. You'll never catch her now," he said.

"Doesn't matter, eh?" Raf said, jerking Sy towards the door. "We'll see about that." A faint smile touched his lips and my stomach lurched.

Kaia

Escaping the spinning blades of the windfarm had meant crawling on my stomach, coughing up dirt. My palms and chin were scraped and there were rips in my tunic. But I'd made it. The need to survive hadn't let me consider what I was doing— only pushed me into action, and now here I was, plodding across the valley.

Nothing Sy had said had prepared me for the hurt of being outside. The dry air burned my lungs. Already, my arms glowed red, sizzling from exposure. And my face, it stung, swollen and itchy. Smearing what I could extract from the aloe leaves helped ease the pain a little, but it dried sticky and stiff. Grains of sand stuck to me, mingling with the salt of my sweat. No matter how much water I drank, my thirst was constant.

I turned back once to see the dome glimmering in the distance. Had my absence been noticed yet? Sari would make excuses for me at work. She'd assume I was still overwrought with grief for Mae and her match with Lev. Had she considered me at all when she agreed to the match with Lev? I was hot and irritated, and her betrayal bit at me. The further I got from the City, the better.

But, eventually, heat and exhaustion won out and I sat down on the scrubby grass that lined the stream and dipped my swollen feet into it. The cool water lapped and sucked at my toes and I thought of Mae's stories about swimming. Reaching into my satchel, I pulled out a papaya, my mouth watering at the thought of the sweet orange flesh. I felt for the knife tucked into my belt but couldn't find it. Had I put it in my satchel?

I pulled out the bedroll, the pot, my drinking gourd, but still no knife. Sy had said it was the most important tool I'd have. It was the one thing I couldn't lose. When had I last used it? An hour ago? Two? With a sinking feeling, I felt the frayed edges of my tunic where I'd sliced a strip off to cover my head from the burning sun. I'd forgotten to put the knife back in my satchel.

With a groan of frustration, I knew I had to go back. I didn't know what waited for me on the Mountain. I needed the knife, but the thought of the satchel digging into my shoulder as I walked back made me want to fall down and cry. Tucking the bag to stay dry among some reedy plants that grew beside the stream, I picked up the drinking gourd and started back the way I'd come.

Lev

Raf wiped a bead of sweat off his brow. "That's it. We've got what we wanted."

Sy lay in a crumpled heap on the floor of a balancing room, moaning. We'd been there for almost an hour. Raf had extracted what information he could from Sy while I watched. I hadn't laid a hand on Sy, but every mark Raf left on him had left one on me too.

I'd lunged once at Raf, begging him to stop. He'd shot me a withering glare and asked if I wanted to be next. "This is part of your training," he'd hissed, shaking me off and continuing. I'd cowered against the wall after that, shutting my eyes at each blow. Finally, Raf opened the door and called to the balancer. "Take him to the infirmary. He had a bad fall."

Sy clutched his stomach and moaned as the balancer lifted him up and forced him to limp across the room. I looked at Raf. At the blood smeared across his cheek. "Come with me."

"Where?"

He threw me a look like I was in no position to be asking. "To tell a Councillor."

"Tell them what? You got the admission by torture. You beat him!"

A cold look crossed his face. "I persuaded."

I stuffed my trembling hands in the pockets of my tunic. "How do we know he didn't lie to make the beating stop?" What would Kaia do if she found out I'd been part of this?

Raf raised an eyebrow. "We don't. But his story didn't change either." He marched to the door and held it open for me. "Let's go."

Tar sat at her desk, swiping her finger with deft movements across her holographic screen. "What?" she barked when we walked in.

"A Citizen is missing. A female," Raf said.

Tar tucked her finger away and the screen wavered and then disappeared. She raised an eyebrow and waited for him to continue.

"She escaped. Went to the Mountain."

I expected Tar to shake her head at the impossibility, like I had. The fact that she didn't sent a cold shiver of dread up my spine.

"Who?"

Raf said nothing.

"Kaia," I whispered.

"How?"

"Through the underland. The male said there's a hatch there that opens up into the windfarm."

Tar's eyes widened at Raf's information. "I see."

"It might not be true. Sy might have lied," I sputtered. "She wouldn't leave—" I caught myself before I finished the sentence, *without me.*

"The male's story didn't change," Raf said. "Even when we pressed him."

Gritting my teeth at the "we," I shot Raf a sidelong glance. What he'd done to Sy, he'd done on his own.

Tar clasped her hands under her chin and inhaled. Her eyes narrowed as she considered the news. "Did he say why she left?"

I glared at Tar, at her feigned ignorance. "You know why—" I started, but Raf cut me off.

"The male we questioned claimed she wasn't right in the head after her elder was balanced."

"Was that all? No mention of any other reason?"

"It was my match with Sari," I blurted. "That was why she left!" All those nights I sat waiting in the orchard for her, giving her time, had been wasted moments. I shouldn't have waited until last night to go to her dwelling. It had already been too late. Tar didn't respond, instead she gave me a cursory glance. "You're dismissed for the day."

I wouldn't let Tar swat me away like I was an annoying insect. "No."

"I beg your pardon?" Tar rose to her feet. "Have you forgotten who you are speaking to?" Her eyes burned when she looked at me. I should have apologized, but I was too angry to back down.

"If she dies, it will be your fault. I'll tell the Council how you tormented her."

Tar took a step closer to me. She had the same look on her face as when she'd crushed the bird in her hand and it made my mouth go dry. My body wanted to run, but for once, I needed to stand strong.

"Leave," Tar said to Raf. I balled my hands into fists and held them at my sides, willing myself to meet her eyes. I flinched when Tar's breath hit my face. "Showing kindness is a luxury that powerful people don't get. It makes you weak. I've tried to teach this to you so many times, but you're too much like Kellan."

Hearing her say his name hit me like a jolt. "What do you mean?"

"Compassion was his downfall."

"So that's why you want to keep me from Kaia? Because you think caring for someone will make me weak?"

"You have no idea who Kaia is. I'm trying to protect you—"

"Protect me from Kaia?" I stared at her incredulously.

"From the City. Don't ask me anymore, Lev," she warned. "There are things about the City you can't know. Not yet."

"What about Kaia?"

"I'll send Raf after her. She has to come back to the City."

"Why?" Nothing she was saying made sense. She'd done everything she could to hurt Kaia, but now she wanted her back and was willing to risk Raf's life to do it.

"Stop asking questions!" Tar took a breath to regain her composure, but I pressed on.

"How will he—?" I thought of Raf's hands on her, doing what he did to Sy and it made vomit rise in my throat. "What if he hurts her?"

"Don't worry. I need her in one piece. Anyway, I have something she'll come back for." A slither of a smile lifted Tar's mouth and with a flick of her finger, she pulled up her hologram and a three-dimensional map of the city appeared.

I followed as she shifted it and zoomed in on the underland. Blinking dots indicated me, Raf, and then further down the tunnel another one. I peered at the name floating above the dot, hardly believing I was seeing it right. Mae.

"I didn't expect she'd prove useful so soon," Tar said.

"Is she really alive?"

"For now."

I stared at Tar and shook my head. "You kept Mae alive? Why?"

"I told you, there are things you can't know. Not yet. But if what you've told me about Kaia is right, she won't gamble with her elder's life."

I swallowed back the hatred for Tar that rose in my gut. "If you think she'll believe Raf, you're wrong." I imagined Kaia wandering, delirious on the scorched valley floor. Suddenly, the solution was clear. "Let me go with him. If I told her about Mae, she'd believe me."

I thought Tar would say no or worse, laugh. "You?" Her eyes, always cold and mirthless, ran over me, appraising. "Hmm.

Interesting. You know outside is unforgiving. There's no room for weakness."

"I know." At least, I thought I did. As crazy as it was to leave the City, I couldn't stay knowing Kaia was out there. Tar thought caring for Kaia made me weak, but the opposite was true. My feelings for Kaia had made me strong.

"It would be a mistake. You'd never survive."

I thought of Kellan and his mission to harness the power of the skies with the kites. The City had never forgotten his sacrifice. He'd become a hero. "Let me go with Raf. Let me prove I can do it."

As the words left my mouth, I realized I'd found a way to beat her at her own game. Tar frowned considering my idea, but I could tell, there was something about it she liked. "How could I send you outside? My own offspring? How would it look to the Council?" Tar asked.

"Like you were raising a leader."

—

Tar hadn't laughed at my idea, but Raf did. As soon as Tar told him. "You aren't serious." His laugh echoed off the walls of her chamber.

"I am," Tar said. "You'll leave immediately."

The laughter died on his lips.

With a sick swell in my stomach, I realized this was happening. "I want to see Mae before I go. I need to know she's alive."

"You're wasting time," she said.

I didn't waver. "You've tricked me before."

"Fine. Follow me." She turned to Raf. "Get your supplies. Be ready to leave when we get back."

Tar and I walked silently down a long stretch of tunnel. We passed a series of doors until we got to one that was unmarked. Tar touched her pulse point to a sensor and pushed it open.

Inside, Mae lay huddled on a mattress, same as the one that had been in the balancing room. The room was dark and Mae squinted into the dim light of the tunnel. "Mae!" I said and rushed to her.

She looked at me, confused.

"It's Lev, Kaia's friend." A slow realization spread across her face.

"Where's Kaia? Do they have her? Is she okay?"

I hesitated between telling her the truth and lying. "Kaia's fine," I said.

"Why am I here? What do they want?" she asked, sobbing. "I should have warned her."

Tar cleared her throat. "Time's up," she said. "You've seen her. She's alive, for now."

Mae peered at Tar's shadowy figure in the doorway. "I have to go, Mae. I'll come back. I promise. And I'll bring Kaia with me."

My stomach churned as I watched Raf unlock the hatch. We were covered head to toe in our white survival suits with only our eyes showing in the small opening in the face mask. The survival suits had been an early answer to surviving the elements, before the City had been completed.

The hatch opened on stiff hinges. A gush of air, hot, dry air from outside flooded in. Raf went first, climbing up and swinging one leg over the edge of the opening. He straddled between the City and the outside for a moment and looked below him. The rope ladder unfurled, banging against the solar panels of the dome. It was a long way down.

Tar stood beside me, watching Raf. He moved down the ladder quickly, hands and feet working in unison. When he was on the ground, she turned to me. "There's no overseer who is

better able to protect you than Raf. Follow his orders, but Lev"—
she gripped my shoulders, forcing me to face her—"*do whatever
it takes to survive.*"

With a deep, anxious breath, I climbed up to the hatch. Tar
had never been kind to me, not the way I'd seen other birth
elders act towards their offspring, but all of a sudden, I felt an
unexpected rush of foreboding. What if I never saw her again?

Tar mistook my hesitation for stalling and took a step back,
as if she needed to put further distance between us. "Go," she
ordered. "Raf is waiting."

I nodded. There were five rungs to climb before my head was
out of the City. For the first time in my life, I wasn't under the
cover of the dome. I blinked. Dry, scorching air bit into my eyes.
Raf was on the ground, waving at me. As if I couldn't see him,
the one figure alone in the vastness of the valley. I looked around.
The Mountain rose in the distance, a hulking beast dominating
the landscape. I'd only ever seen it through the dome, but to look
at it from outside gave me new perspective. We were to climb it,
find Kaia and return. There could be Prims, beasts, storms, and
dangers I'd never considered. What if we ran out of water? Were
injured? What if the survival suits didn't work?

I took another shaky breath. It was too late to turn back. I
didn't have a choice. I had to go down to meet Raf. *Think about
Kaia*, I reminded myself. If Sy was telling the truth, she was out
here somewhere, unprotected and alone.

With that thought, I swung my legs over the hatch and began
my descent. The ladder scraped against the dome, shifting side
to side as I climbed. I was slower than Raf, cautious. I imagined
his eyes on me, judging. Weighing my value as a partner.

"You made it," he said when I jumped to the ground beside him.
My arms and legs trembled from fear or exertion, maybe both.

I nodded, adjusted the pack slung over my back and looked

to him for direction. "Let's go," he said grimly and turned in the direction of the Mountain. We had to walk around the City, away from the lightning conductors with the kites that snapped in the wind. I looked up to the hatch and saw Tar watching. She raised her hand, waved goodbye and then turned away.

Kaia

I was sure I'd gone too far, wasting steps towards the City when I should have been going in the opposite direction. I could have walked past the knife. There was nothing to identify where I'd been when I'd stopped, no rock or tree; everything outside looked the same.

But then I did see something. The glint of metal. At first I thought it was my eyes playing tricks on me, but as I got closer, I saw that it was my knife. I raced to it, falling on the ground and laughing. I held the knife in my hands. Gripping it. Grateful. The sheath lay in the reeds. Clutching both of them to my chest, I promised myself I wouldn't be so foolish again.

I began the long walk back to my satchel. How much time had I lost? An hour at least? And another hour back to where I'd started.

Movement in the sky made me look up. A bird, enormous compared to any we had in the City, soared overhead. I arched my neck, watching as it circled and swooped. Its wings were as wide as I was tall. It let out a caw and suddenly it dove. Its beak trained on me, aiming. I screamed and fell to the ground, curled up, covering my neck with my hands. The bird took a pass over my back. I felt the whoosh of wind.

Uncovering my head, I peeked at the sky. The bird was circling back. Its talons were the size of my head. The only weapon I had was my knife. Pulling it out of the sheath, I held it tight, sweat making the handle slippery. The bird cawed again, tri-umphant. A streak of black in the sky, it circled again and dove. I flipped over, my knife ready. As the bird came close, its beak slicing through the air, I swung madly. A flurry of feathers, a high-pitched squawk and the bird flapped away. Uninjured, but stunned. It hadn't expected me to fight. Scrambling up, I took off my sandals, held them in one hand and started to do the one thing that was as natural to me as breathing. I ran.

The heat and sun were forgotten as muscle memory kicked in. My body, sinewy and strong from years of daily runs, sprang into action. The bird circled in the sky, ready to swoop and attack. It was waiting for me to stumble, to weaken.

I won't, I thought as my feet pounded the scrubby grass along the stream. *I can't.*

Lev

The survival suits had made me feel invincible when we first stepped outside. But the longer we trudged, the more cumber-some they became. Worse even than overseer tunics. I'd done the calculations. If Sy was telling the truth, we'd left four hours behind Kaia. Raf estimated the walk across the valley to be six hours, based on what, I didn't know. He'd never been outside either and he'd never been to the Mountain, but I accepted what he said without argument. If his calculations were right, Kaia would be over halfway to the Mountain by now. Or she could be passed out on the sun-baked ground, burnt and dehydrated. Forcing the rising panic back down, I picked up the pace. Finding her was all that mattered.

"You were close with her, this female?" Raf asked when we'd been walking for an hour. The sun was directly overhead, and even through the survival suit, I could feel its intensity.

"Yes."

"Did you want to be matched with her?"

"Yes."

Raf turned to me and I expected him to mock me, but instead his voice turned serious. "It's hard to lose the one you want."

"You're speaking from experience?"

"Maybe." He didn't say anything else and I knew better than to ask.

Raf glanced back. A bank of low, dark clouds scuttled across the sky. "That storm's moving fast," he muttered. He plowed forward as the wind picked up. It took effort to keep pace with him.

I'd seen plenty of storms hit before, but always from inside the safety of the dome. The thought of being outside when one came was terrifying. "What do we do when it hits?"

"Keep moving. Maybe the female will realize how impossible it is to survive out here. Maybe she'll turn around."

And then we could all go back to the City. Kaia could be reunited with Mae. I would break off the match with Sari and somehow convince Tar, and the matchmakers, that Kaia and I should be together.

"See that?" Raf pointed to the sky. In the distance a black bird circled. "That's a bird of prey. Its talons are like knives. Probably found her before we did. It'll kill her and then pick her bones clean. Won't be anything left for us to take home but her tunic."

I gritted my teeth against his words. He was enjoying the torment they caused me.

His pace quickened. "No one can survive out here on their own."

Despite my hopes for the opposite, I was starting to think he was right.

Kaia

The knife attack had kept the bird a safe distance away from me. It kept circling as I trudged towards my satchel, but knew better than to attack again.

I longed for the safety of the City.

Thinking about the City made me think of Sy. I fought the wave of emotion that rolled through me. I couldn't waste water on tears.

My satchel was waiting for me where I left it. I hitched it up on my shoulder, and the weight felt comforting now, not as much of a burden. I kept walking. My legs ached but the Mountain was almost in reach. I turned back and scanned the horizon. The City was so far behind me it was just a bump on the valley floor. Behind it, storm clouds moved with menacing speed across the sky. In minutes, they would engulf the valley and release a torrent of rain. There was something else in the distance. I squinted. Was I imagining it? Two figures in white. My breath caught in my throat.

They'd come after me.

A rumble shook the ground. Flashes of sheet lightning lit up the sky, bruising the swollen grey clouds to purple. My exhaustion forgotten, I ran for the safety of the Mountain.

I was too afraid to look back as I scrambled uphill. There were trees now, their prickly branches tore at my skin. An animal, furry with long ears, darted out from behind a bush and ran in front of me. With a startled scream, I fell, banging my knee hard on a rock. I felt a hot trickle of blood run down my shin but didn't look at it. I kept going, using my hands to scrabble up the slope. Lunging for the trees, I dragged myself up and hid under their branches.

When I looked back down, I was surprised how high I'd climbed. I had a view of the valley below. And the two figures

that were following me. A crack of thunder echoed. A few angry
drops of rain pummelled the ground. And then the clouds opened
and the rain came down fast, in hard-edged slaps.

I had to keep moving. There was only one reason the overseers were outside and it was to find me. Veering to the right,
away from the stream, I wound my way through the trees, wishing for flat ground so I could catch my breath. But the trees only
grew denser as I climbed higher. The trees scratched my skin and
tore holes in my tunic. The hem lay in tatters, chunks of fabric
missing, tangled in the prickly needles, and I'd lost my headscarf.
The bamboo sandals had saved my feet, but they did nothing to
deter the clouds of insects waiting for me to slow down so they
could feast on me. Sweat ran down my forehead and neck.

As I climbed, the rain stopped, replaced with a blanket of
mist. I looked back down the Mountain once to see if the overseers were close, but all I could see were trees. Endless trees. And
they all looked identical. The path I'd just climbed had already
been swallowed up, concealed by branches and trunks. I listened
for the stream, but heard nothing.

Sy had told me to stay by the stream. But I'd veered off course
and now I was lost. And then, from high in the treetops, the caw
of that stupid, monstrous bird. Could it get through the trees to
attack? I was weak and exhausted. The gash in my knee throbbed;
a rivulet of blood trickled down my mud-covered leg. Every cell
of my skin screamed with the sting of the sun. With a panicked
sob, I sank to the ground.

Let the overseers find me, I thought. This plan was madness,
hatched in a moment of weakness. I should go back down the
Mountain and give myself up to the overseers. I'd accept whatever
punishment awaited me in the City.

But then another thought: I'd made it this far. Despite the
obstacles of leaving the City without Sy and crossing the valley,

I'd arrived at the Mountain. I'd done what I thought was impossible. If I gave up now, it meant the City had won again. With newfound resolve, I stood up.

A smell, not foul, but musky and salty, carried on the air. I caught a whiff of it before a hand clamped over my mouth and I was dragged away.

Lev

Raf froze and held his hand out for me to do the same. His gaze landed somewhere at the base of Mountain. "Did you see that?" he asked, turning to face me. The Mountain stretched in front of us like a wall. The storm clouds hovered above, ready to unleash the storm.

"There was movement, just below the trees."

I looked at where he pointed, doubtful. "It could have been an animal, or—"

"A Prim," he finished for me. "It wasn't. It was her."

I wanted to believe him, but how could he be so sure? How could he tell the difference between Kaia and a Prim at this distance? I didn't get to ask because a loud crack shook the ground. The clouds burst open and rain pelted down.

"Keep moving!" Raf shouted, as if we had a choice. There was no place to take shelter; we wouldn't reach the Mountain before the storm hit. All we could do was walk, heads bowed, shoulders hunched, and hope it would pass quickly. There was no way to control the storm; the elements were unforgiving.

Kaia! I called in my head. *How will you survive this?*

⏑

"Yaw!" Raf, held his arms out and hollered at the sky in triumph. The last few drops had fallen and the sky was lightening. "Yaw!"

he shouted again. We'd made it through the storm, sometimes huddling against each other as the wind battered against us. Outside had done its worst and we'd survived. The Mountain was within reach.

My canteen dangled from one hand as I threw my head back and shouted with abandon. Raf laughed as my voice echoed off the Mountain and slapped my shoulder. "We did it!" he congratulated me. The stream, full with rain water, tumbled frothy over rocks.

"I have to fill up my canteen," I said and let my pack drop to the ground.

The sudden stop made my pulse point flicker with static. Raf had warned me that as we got further from the City, the signal would weaken. There had already been intermittent buzzing in my ear, like a nagging insect.

"If it was her I saw before the storm hit, we're gaining on her," he said, looking up at the Mountain and its mass of green. "But she could be anywhere on this Mountain. It'll be hard-going when night comes. I figure we have a couple more hours. Once the sun goes down, it'll get dark quickly."

"Where will we sleep?" I asked as I dipped my canteen, a relic from the original inhabitants, into the stream. The water gurgled as it flowed through the built-in purifier.

"We won't. Best plan is to keep moving, try to gain some ground on her." Raf surveyed the space around him. He was different out here, some of his overseer arrogance had worn away.

"What if the Prims find her first?" I asked. I hated to think it, but it was possible. We were on their territory now. And alone and unarmed, I wondered what chance Kaia had against the Prims.

"I don't know what they'd do if they found her. They aren't like us," Raf said.

"How do you know?" I hadn't meant it to be a challenge, but

by the way he answered, with clipped words, I knew he'd taken it that way.

"I've met some."

"When?"

"A long time ago," he said. "We caught some and brought them into the City."

My mouth hung open. Prims had been in the City?

"I thought they'd be wild, you know?" Raf raised his hands and made a comically fierce growl. "But they weren't. They were angry they'd been captured and worried about their families. They wanted to go back to the Mountain."

"What do you mean captured?"

"They came looking for something. After years of them keeping to themselves, they showed up. We let them come in, but we didn't let them go. That's all I know."

"What happened?"

Raf shrugged. "I was moved to a different post. My guess is that they were balanced."

I shook my head, confused. "The City captured them and then killed them? Why?"

Instead of answering, he clipped his water bottle onto his pack. "Might be a good idea to keep your knife handy. Who knows what's hiding in the trees."

I pulled the knife out of its holster. With a long blade and thick bamboo handle, it was the heaviest one I'd ever held. I kept it gripped in my hand, my eyes darting in every direction.

"We're going uphill now," Raf said. "Pace yourself." The slope was so steep that I had to hold on to tree branches to make my way further up the Mountain.

Raf's strides grew longer as the incline got steeper. The danger that lay ahead didn't faze him, he seemed eager to embrace it, forging ahead. No wonder Tar had told me to follow his commands. But she'd also said *Do whatever it takes to survive.* What if the two things worked against each other?

I switched the knife to my left hand, letting the circulation flow back into the fingers of my right hand. I stopped and looked around, if only to prove to myself that the spine-tingling feeling that we weren't alone was just my imagination.

Kaia

I struggled. I tried to bite the hand covering my mouth. I kicked at the ground, dragging my heels. The overseers were too far away to hear me, but I screamed anyway. The muffled sound was lost as I was pulled into a cave.

"Shhhh," a voice said. A male. He eased his grip over my mouth. My fight weakened as he pulled me deeper into the cave. It smelled damp, the air murky and festering with fungus and moss, life that fed off gloom.

Another male, younger, emerged from the darkness. A fire burned in the centre. I stared at it, mesmerized. Mae had told me about fire. The idea of it had filled me with fear. She'd told me it could be started by lightning and how entire forests had burned down. But this fire crackled and flickered, warming the walls of the cave. A grey mist, like heavy steam from boiling water, rose up from it.

"Don't scream," the male said and took his hand off my mouth. I couldn't, even if I'd wanted to: my throat was dry with fear.

The younger one squatted and rested his elbows on his knees. He poked at the burning sticks with another, longer stick. The end was blackened and sharp. He kept stealing sidelong glances at me, an anxious furrow in his brow.

"Who are you?" I whispered. The male passed me my canteen and held it in front of my lips. With a wary glance at them, I grabbed it and took a sip. Smoke had started to fill the cave. It burned my eyes. I looked up, realizing for the first time how enormous the room was. Tunnels led off in different directions.

"I don't think you're in a position to ask questions, do you?" He peered down at me. The firelight flickered off the hollows and peaks on his face, his skin dark as aged resin. Shaggy dark hair hung limp and matted on his head, like an overgrown plant. A beard trailed to his chest.

I licked my lips, wishing for more water but afraid to ask. The knives in their belts glinted in the dim light. As discreetly as possible, I felt for mine and then spotted it lying on the ground beside the younger one.

"What's your name?"

"Kaia."

He narrowed his eyes at me. "You left the City? When?"

I hesitated, unsure if he could be trusted. He hadn't asked me to follow him, he'd captured me. I wasn't a guest, I was a prisoner. "This morning. Before sunrise."

"Alone?" The younger one asked. His skin was sun-baked too, and he had a beard, but it was trimmed and not so wild looking.

I nodded. It wasn't a lie. I had left alone, and I grit my teeth against mentioning the overseers I'd seen in the valley. What if the Prims were hostile? I might need the overseers. A forced return to the City might be the lesser of two evils.

"Why?" The older one's eyes dug into me.

It was too much to explain. Words failed me. I stared at him, despondent. "I can't live there anymore."

He grunted and reached for my hand. I tried to jerk it away, but he held it tightly. His fingers were calloused like Sy's, and filthy. Rubbing a finger over my pulse point, he clucked at me. "They're tracking you."

I shook my head. "It's broken. No one knows I left." Except Sy, another secret I wouldn't divulge.

The younger one leaned in. "I've never seen one," he muttered and rubbed his thumb over my pulse point. "So, this controls them?" he asked his friend.

"No!" I snatched my hand back, indignant. "It records energy production." The two of them exchanged glances of disbelief.

"Can you make it do something?"

I lifted my finger, expecting a hologram to appear, but nothing happened. Lowering it, I tried again and stared at the cave wall. My whole life, a hologram had appeared with a flick of my finger, connecting me with the rest of the City and displaying my memories. But now, that was gone too. "See," I said shakily, "it's not working." I caught the skeptical look that passed between them. "It's true," I said, fearful that they wouldn't believe me. "It's how I escaped."

Neither of them said anything, but a look passed between them, like I wasn't to be believed. The younger one bent closer, inspecting my knee. "What happened?"

"I fell," I answered. Dirt covered my knee and was embedded in the trail of congealed blood that ran down my leg. The cut had started to bleed again.

The older one made a noise in his throat. "It'll get infected."

They looked at each other again and frowned. "We should get her to camp. Make her comfortable."

Confused by the ominous tone of the older one's voice, I watched as they dipped long sticks into the fire. The flames shot out at the cave walls. I ducked, cowering away. The younger one kicked dirt onto the fire in the centre until it died. He picked up my knife and slid it into a sash at his waist. He saw me watching. "Just keeping it safe for you," he said.

The older one surveyed me with a smirk and held out his hand to pull me up. "I'm Akrum. This is Gideon," he pointed to the younger one who held his fire stick higher so the firelight flickered across his eyes. They were kind and curious and for a moment, I forgot to be scared. "You've made Gideon's day. He's always wanted to meet a refugee fresh from the City."

So that was what I was, a refugee?

Gideon's shoulders filled the narrow tunnel and when he moved, I could see the power of his body, well-muscled limbs used to the harsh conditions of life on the Mountain, so different from the lithe, slim figures of Citizens. With no protection on the Mountain, Akrum and Gideon's skin looked as weather-beaten as the valley. Mae had told me that the solar panels on the dome filtered out the harmful spectrum of sunlight and made natural pigment unnecessary. After years of living in the City, every Citizen had a version of the same silvery, pale skin. I looked weak and vulnerable compared to both of them. "It's a long walk through the cave tunnels, but still a shortcut. Are you coming with us?"

It was an invitation, not a threat. I hesitated. Their appearance and roughness was intimidating, and Akrum put me on edge; his gaze was harsh. But if they were going to hurt me, wouldn't they have done it already? Gideon waited impatiently at the forking tunnels and held out a torch to his friend. What choice did I have? Go back to the Mountain, lost and wounded, and wander? Or let the overseers capture me? If I wanted to find Raina, following these Prims was my best chance. With a brusque nod, I ignored his hand, got to my feet and limped after them.

The tunnel narrowed and we had to stoop until it opened up again into another large chamber and then we took a different path that twisted and turned. I reached out a tentative hand. The stone was cool and rough. A knot of fear tightened in my belly. I was following these people deeper into the cave. What if they weren't Prims, but some other group?

They both stopped suddenly and looked up. A hole opened at

the top of the cave and I could see daylight. Akrum held his torch up high, whistling like a bird. Seconds later, a rope ladder was dropped down. It swung in front of us. Gideon began to climb, the ladder swinging side to side as he made his way up. "Your turn," Akrum said. He held both torches and his face glowed orange, a lopsided smile showed yellowing, decayed teeth.

I stared at the ladder, gripped both sides of the rope and tested the bottom rung with my foot. With a deep breath, I took a step up, the narrow rope pressing into the sole of my sandals. The ladder swung for a sickening moment until Akrum grabbed it, securing it below me. I moved up, hand over hand. I looked down once and my stomach lurched at how far I'd climbed.

The smell of fresh air replaced the dank, still air of the cave. I put one arm on the ledge and hauled my body up, rolling out of the way and scrambling to my feet. At least thirty Prims stared at me. They stood in a semi-circle and began to hiss. It was a horrible sound, filling my ears as they advanced. I shrank back searching for Gideon.

"Stop!" he said barging in front of me. "She's not going to hurt us!"

The hissing died out, but the hostile looks didn't. "How do you know?" a female said.

Akrum leaped over the edge, his agility surprising for someone of his age.

"Did you remove it?" The female's voice was sharp with suspicion. Two braids of red hair, as thick as hemp ropes, hung on either side of her face.

Remove what? I wondered.

"Show them," he commanded me and gave my finger a pointed look. When I raised it, they all leaned away from me. I didn't know what they thought would appear, knives that would fly through the air at them? A flock of birds to carry them away?

But there was an audible sigh of relief when nothing happened. "The thing in her finger is broken."

The female, a few years older than me, ran her eyes up and down me, staring hard at my face. "She could be lying."

I looked to Akrum, but he said nothing in my defence. "I'm not lying," I whispered.

"That's what you'd say if you were," she sneered. "Was she armed?"

"She had a knife," Akrum said. "Gideon took it." A low murmur ran through them.

"I'm not here to hurt you," I said, my voice shaking. Was one of them Raina? I looked at the crowd, searching each face for one that looked like the female in Mae's memory.

"Why are you here then?" A large male, maybe the tallest human I'd ever seen, piped up. His deep voice silenced all the other questions.

"I can't live there anymore." My voice cracked, more from exhaustion than emotion.

Gideon stared at the others angrily. "Look at her, would you? She's no threat to us. Anyway, she's got a wound on her knee."

His words seemed to calm their fears. The female with braids gave a disgruntled sigh and muttered something to the big male. One by one, they turned and left the clearing, walking single file down a forest path. "I'll tell the Chief," Gideon said to Akrum. Before he left, he gave me a long look. I met his gaze and then turned away, unsettled.

"Why do they hate me?" I asked.

"They're afraid. We haven't had a refugee in a long time," Akrum said.

"There've been others?" My breath quickened at the thought of Raina. Had she made it?

"A few, over the years."

"A few?" I repeated, turning to him in surprise.

He nodded and drew his eyebrows together in a frown as he looked at my knee. "I never told the other refugees what would come, when we found them." He sighed. "But, I'm old now," he grimaced. "And wiser." He drew me closer and lowered his voice. "You're going to die on this Mountain, Kaia."

I stared at him.

"Death is coming for you. And there's nothing you can do to stop it."

Lev

We'd stopped for another break. Thankfully. Raf's pace was punishing and sweat dripped down my back. My shoulders had been rubbed raw from carrying the backpack. The storm had left the ground slippery and spatters of mud covered our suits. I looked up at the cloudless sky. Raf kept reminding me how few daylight hours we had until night fell. I swatted at the clouds of insects buzzing around my head. Nothing in my overseer training had prepared me for being outside. I wondered how Kaia was managing. Even without Mae's life at stake, I was sure Kaia would agree to come back to the City when we found her. She must have discovered by now that whatever she'd fled hadn't been as bad as what she was running to.

What was she running to, anyway? What did she think she'd find on the Mountain?

I couldn't shake the feeling that Tar knew more about Kaia than she had let on. After all, she'd taken Mae prisoner before Kaia had left. Why? What did Kaia have that Tar wanted? And why did she need to use Mae to get it? I was missing something, but what?

"How did Tar know to take Mae? Did she know Kaia was going to leave?" I finally asked.

Raf didn't answer right away. He grabbed a stick off the ground and twirled it between his fingers. I watched as he pulled a knife out of his belt and shaved bits off the end, whittling it to a point.

"Tar must have told you," I pressed. "She tells you everything."

"Tar and I have known each other our whole lives. We were classmates, me, her and Kellan, then trained as overseers together."

"Was she always so—"

"Menacing? No. Not always. She got that way after Kellan died. His death made her see things differently. She had you to look after and set her eyes on the Council. Her happiness didn't matter anymore." Raf stopped talking and sniffed the air. "Do you smell that?"

I raised my nose, but all I could smell was the sharp tang of the forest. Raf tucked his knife away, put on his pack and signalled for me to do the same. He took a few steps forward, then a few more. I got up to follow him, wondering how far we'd let his nose take us. When he stopped, I looked to where he was pointing. At his feet was a pile of excrement. I curled my nose in distaste, but he peered at it, intrigued.

"You don't know what this is, do you?"

I resisted the urge to roll my eyes. "A pile of—"

"It's not human," he interrupted. "It's from a beast."

I watched him, not sure if he was making fun of me. "They're real?"

Raf nodded. "They were bred to protect the City and keep the Prims away. Some kind of hybrid. They were pack animals, excellent hunters and intensely protective of their territory. They were too smart though. When there wasn't enough food, the alpha led his pack away from the City."

"And came here." I stared at the pile of dung. "How do you know it's theirs"

"I don't. I'm guessing." Raf took a long look around, spinning to get a 360 degree view.

"Is it fresh?"

Raf jabbed at it with his walking stick. The point sank in. "A few hours, maybe. We should get moving." He adjusted his pack and waited for me to do the same. "Keep your eyes open. If it's not the beasts, it could be something else. Maybe more dangerous."

A lump of fear rose in my throat. *More dangerous?*

Raf started to walk, moving branches out of the way with his stick, his boots leaving indentations in the tall grass along the stream.

I glanced over my shoulder. The feeling that we were being watched hadn't left me. And now there was the added fear of night coming.

Up ahead, on the other side of the stream, among the deep greens and browns of the forest, a fragment of pale fabric dangled off the end of a branch. "Raf," I said. He turned and looked where I pointed.

We waded across the stream, slowly and then faster, splashing with excitement. Raf got to it first, fingered its familiarity, and held it out to me. A piece of a Citizen's tunic, the fabric unmistakable. A grin stretched across his face. He crumpled the fabric in his hand, shaking it with triumph.

But I didn't feel triumphant. My stomach dropped. It was proof. She'd really left.

Without me.

How had she managed to get this far on her own? Without any protective gear, wearing only a Citizen's tunic? Beasts, Prims, storms, insects; the Mountain teemed with dangers. With a renewed vigour, I realized I was Kaia's only hope. Unless we found her, she'd die out here.

Raf was already barging through the branches, forging deeper into the forest, following a trail visible only to him. "This way," he said with confidence. I turned back once to see the stream disappearing behind us, swallowed up by trees.

—

I collapsed to the ground, resting against a rotted log, too tired to swat at the insects flying around my head. Raf pulled some dried papaya from his pack and tossed it at my feet. Bright orange and tough, it softened up as I sucked on the end of it. We hadn't spoken much as we walked for the last two hours, both of us on edge. The sky had gone from blue to violet and was now bleeding into black.

I held up my finger and waited for my hologram to appear. Weak and flickering, it floated in front of me for a minute and then disappeared. My thoughts went briefly to the City. What was going on there without me? Had anyone noticed I wasn't at my usual posts? Had Sari? I felt a twinge of guilt that I hadn't told her I was leaving, or why.

"The last record of her in the City was over a week ago, did you know that?" Raf asked, interrupting my thoughts.

"That's not possible. She was at the gymnasium every day until her elder was balanced."

"She might have been at the gymnasium, but her joules were never recorded, or used. She went dark eight days ago."

"Went dark?"

"Her pulse point malfunctioned. At least, that's what I figure happened."

"She'd have told me if something was wrong," I said.

"She didn't tell you she was running away," he pointed out.

I thought back to our last night together in the orchard after the energy-sharing rule was announced. With a wince, I remembered it had been me who'd suggested running away.

"You'll need your lightstick now," Raf said and pulled one out of his pack before looping the straps around his shoulders.

Moments after he spoke, the last bit of light left the sky and the Mountain was plunged into darkness. "We have to keep going."

I pulled my lightstick out too. Powered by our bodies' electrical impulses, it cast a weak beam of light over the ground. I stood up with a groan and stuffed the papaya away. We made our way slowly, keeping the gurgle of the stream close. There was one positive to the darkness: the Prims were as trapped by the night as we were.

It was slow-going with our lightsticks. Their glow only lit up a small circle at our feet, but Raf was right, it was better to be moving. As tired as I was, I wanted to find Kaia and start back to the City. The less time I had to spend outside, the better. I swore I'd never complain about the boredom of life in the City again.

But as the hours passed and the sky brightened, we found no more signs of Kaia. Trepidation filled me and I started to echo Raf's mumbled thoughts. *We should have found her by now.*

"We should talk," Raf said, surprising me. "To fight off exhaustion. It will keep us alert."

"Did someone go after the other Citizens who left?" I asked.

"We never needed to. By the time we figured out they were gone, their bodies had shown up."

"What do you mean 'bodies'?"

"The Prims brought them back in the night. Dumped them outside the dome. We didn't know if they were killing them, or finding them already dead."

I stared at him, astonished. "They all died?"

"Citizens can't survive outside of the dome. After living in the City for so long, we've lost immunity to the bacteria and germs. An infected cut or insect bite is deadly. None of the Citizens who left had these," he pointed to his survival suit. "The Prims though, their bodies have adapted. That's what got us thinking, we needed to study Prim blood."

Study Prim blood? I frowned at Raf. He wasn't making sense. Maybe exhaustion had finally caught up with him.

"But first we had to get some Prims."

I laughed, assuming he was joking.

He wasn't.

"Kellan saw them one day, tramping across the valley. We sent out a convoy who reported the Prims were asking for help. There was a sickness on the Mountain and they needed medicine. We agreed, let them in, and then didn't let them out."

"There were Prims in the City?"

Raf nodded.

"What did you do with them?" I almost tripped over a tree root, I was so preoccupied with the conversation.

Raf didn't answer. He stopped walking and leaned on his walking stick, breathing heavily. "Raf?" He blinked and looked at me confused. "Raf? Are you okay?"

He put a hand to his head. "It's starting," he muttered. "Are you getting them? These dizzy spells?" I held up my lightstick. His face had a sickly pallor to it and there were dark circles under his eyes.

"Maybe you should sleep? I can keep watch. We've been on the move for almost twenty-four hours."

Raf shook his head. "We can rest when we find the female."

I waited until he'd had a sip of water and looked more alert to ask about the rest of his story. "You were telling me about Prims in the City," I prompted.

He frowned. "I was?"

"The City had captured some," I let my voice drift off and hoped he'd pick up the story.

"The City didn't capture them. Kellan did," he corrected. "It was his idea," he snorted, remembering. "Once he got an idea in his head, there was no stopping him. They did all kinds of tests and in the end, figured out that over the years the Prims' genetics had evolved. Their blood carried an immunity ours didn't."

I'd learned about genetics and biological evolution in school. It made sense that the Prims would have adapted to survive outside. But I didn't know how all of this related to Kaia.

"The leader of the experiment wanted to take it a step further. She implanted an embryo fertilized by a Prim into herself. She wanted to see if interbreeding would create a stronger species capable of living outside."

I stared at him, my mouth hanging open. How could all these things have gone on in the City, hidden from Citizens? "Did it work?"

His eyes locked on mine. "If we find Kaia, and she's still alive, then yes."

Kaia

Akrum's words echoed in my head as he led me through the trees to the Prims' camp. "You're trying to scare me," I shot back at him, forcing myself to stay calm.

He shook his head and pointed to the gash on my knee. "It will kill you. You have no immunity to the germs and bacteria that exist outside your City." There was no animosity in his voice, but his words still stabbed, ripping into my chest. I stared at my knee, imagining miniscule bacteria writhing inside the cut, needling their way into my bloodstream. The bug bites had turned into red, itchy bumps on my legs, arms and neck. Was their poison deadly to me too?

I swallowed, trying to still my trembling hands. My blood had betrayed me. Again. How much time did I have? Hours? Days? "Why didn't you just leave me to die?"

"Ask Gideon," was all he said. "If it's any comfort, when you die, we will return your body to the City. You should be with your people."

I gave him a strange look, not understanding. There was no reason to be returned. Balanced Citizens were incinerated, their ashes mixed into cement. Why would Prims risk their lives to return a body?

I dropped my pack. "I came here to find someone. A female named Raina."

Akrum shook his head. "We have no Raina here."

It took a moment for his words to sink in. *We have no Raina here,* echoed in my head. Of course there wasn't. Sy was a fool and I was an idiot for believing him. I was too exhausted to cry. Leaving the City had been pointless.

Akrum picked up my bag and gestured for me to follow. "Come. You need to eat." He gave my knee a doubtful look, "Our healer might be able to help. Make you more comfortable, at least, when the fever sets in."

I closed my eyes and ignored him. I couldn't face the Prims and their menacing looks. What if they hissed at me as I walked through camp? Akrum tried cajoling me, but I sank to the ground. He lifted my elbow and tried to drag me, but I fought back and he gave up. "Suit yourself," he said with a resigned sigh. "It'll be dark in a couple of hours. Camp's that way." He pointed down the path the other Prims had taken and then left.

I huddled with my satchel, wishing I still had my knife. I trusted the Prims as much as they trusted me. I'd seen the looks on their faces. They'd as soon slit my throat as welcome me into their camp. I was the enemy.

But worse, there was no Raina. I'd left the City to chase a dream and now I'd die for it.

"Kaia!" Gideon crouched over me, light from his torch flickering across his face.

"You need to come to camp. It's dangerous for you to stay out here," he whispered. I woke up with a start, remembering where I was. I hadn't meant to fall asleep. I sat up and hugged my knees to my chest, inching away from Gideon. "Why did Akrum leave you here?" he asked, annoyance flaring in his voice.

"It was my choice. I didn't want to go into camp."

"Why not?"

"I know I'm going to die," I mumbled, pulling away from him. "The cut on my knee will get infected."

He moved the bandage and took a closer look at my knee. Heat from the torch warmed my skin. "It doesn't look any worse. Come on, let's get you to camp."

I didn't move. The hiss of the Prims when they'd seen me still echoed in my head. They looked wild and intimidating with their dirty faces, long hair and patchwork clothing; barely human compared with the clean, pale, almost hairless Citizens. The Prims radiated something feral, like they were part of the earth itself. I longed for the sterile City, with its protective dome, and for my sleeping capsule, warm and soft. With all my heart, I wished I'd never left the City. I silently cursed Sy and his plan, and myself for being desperate enough to listen to him.

Gideon's voice softened. "We can wait here until camp is quiet, okay? Not everyone is afraid of you. Although it was kind of funny watching Big Sam's face when you held up your finger. I've never seen him so scared. He looked like he was going to piss his pants."

I didn't find anything funny about it. Gideon jammed the torch into the earth. "I'll sit with you," he said.

Having him close calmed me. The noise of the camp filtered through the trees. "*They're* afraid of *me*?

"Not of you, exactly, City people in general." There was a long pause.

"What about the female with the red hair? She looked like she wanted to kick me back down the hole."

Gideon turned somber. "Nadia's been through a lot. It's just her and her two brothers now."

"And Sam?"

"Big Sam? Lost his best friend. He's never forgiven himself."

I didn't see what any of that had to do with me or the City. Maybe Sy had been wrong and the Prims were still bitter about being turned away generations ago. *I've lost people too*, I wanted to tell Gideon. Prims aren't the only ones who've been hurt. "I didn't come here to make enemies. I came looking for someone but Akrum told me she's not here. She never was here."

"I'm sorry," Gideon said. "You left for nothing."

I swallowed back a lump in my throat. "Yeah." I turned away so he couldn't see my tears. "We're taught to fear you," I said, sniffling.

He gave a wry smile. "And? Are we terrifying?"

Yes! screamed in my head, but I didn't say it out loud. Besides Gideon, the rest of them terrified me.

On the other side of the trees, the camp settled in for the night. Fires died and conversations ended. "Tell me about the thing in your finger," Gideon asked. "How does it work?"

Talking about my pulse point wasn't what I wanted to do, but it was a distraction. So, I began explaining about 'Energy In Equals Energy Out' and the gymnasium. He asked about my family and friends, but I couldn't bring myself to tell him about Sari and Lev. Instead I told him about games Lev and I played as children, floating boats on the stream and running from bridge to bridge to see whose had won.

"Is Lev your brother?" he asked.

I shook my head. "No."

"A friend?" Gideon prodded.

He had been more than a friend.

Gideon tilted his head at me. I picked up a small pebble. Worn smooth, it settled comfortably in my hand. I thought about Mae and the pain of losing her. I looked at Gideon. We were nearly the same age, yet his life as a Prim had toughened him. He exuded strength and confidence unlike anyone in the City.

"I know it didn't seem like it at first, but you're safe here," he said quietly. "I promise."

I let his words fill up the empty holes left by Lev and Mae. And Sy, who'd sent me outside unprepared, filled with false hope.

"Come," Gideon said, picking up the torch. "It's quiet." He was right. He reached his hand out to me. Momentarily dizzy when I stood up, I grabbed it. His grip was firm and reassuring, but unfamiliar. As soon as I was on my feet, I let my hand drop, trying to ignore the lingering warmth of his touch. He let me move ahead of him as the path narrowed, one hand resting on the small of my back, guiding me. My back stiffened at his touch.

Stumbling into the clearing behind Gideon, I looked at my surroundings. The scent of wood smoke was heavy in the air and a few fires still smoldered. Thirty shelters ringed the open area. By the light of Gideon's torch, I wondered how buildings made with such a variety of materials stayed standing. Stones stuck together with hardened mud formed the base, and above that, logs and things salvaged from before made the walls.

Only one fire remained lit. As Gideon walked towards it, I fell back, watching. There were four people sitting around it, perched on logs and rough-hewn chairs. They were shadows, their faces cloaked in darkness, the flame sputtering against their legs.

"Gideon!" A man, older, ruddy-skinned, with wiry arms and legs, came forward and embraced him.

I hugged my arms to my chest and stayed hidden in the dark. He came towards me until he stood an arm's length away. Gideon held his torch up high and I saw the lines carved in his face, around his eyes and along his mouth. Unruly hairs shot out from his eyebrows, some grey, some black. He looked unkempt and slightly mad.

"What's your name?"

My pulse quickened. Their attention made me nervous.

"Kaia," I whispered.

"I am Chief Ezekiel, the leader." He moved towards me quickly and grabbed my wrist, pulling my hand up to his ear. I tried to yank it away, but his grip was strong, the tendons in his arms taut with the effort. Holding my four fingers down, he raised my index finger to his ear.

"It's broken," I said. But even if it wasn't, a pulse point wasn't like a heart. It didn't make a sound. There was no point in explaining this because he silenced me with a look, his bushy eyebrows furrowing together as he listened.

"Can they track you?" he asked.

I shook my head and kept quiet about the overseers in the valley. They'd have made it to the Mountain by now, but finding me would be almost impossible. Even with months of searching, they might never locate the Prim camp tucked away in the trees. I guess I'd been lucky that Gideon and Akrum had found me, otherwise I'd be wandering too.

He frowned and he sighed. "But, you don't know. None of the refugees *know*. You come to us, seeking refuge, but care nothing for the harm that might follow." While he'd been talking, Gideon moved to my side. I shifted closer to him, wondering if the Chief could sense my dishonesty.

"She's hurt," Gideon said.

The Chief's eyes flickered over to him. "Akrum told me." He

bent down to examine my knee. He motioned for the torch to be lowered and held it so close to my tunic that I worried it would catch fire. The flame licked and twisted. And then his hands were on my leg, warm and rough, like dried leaves, turning it to get a better view. I held my jaw tight with distaste, wishing he'd get his filthy hands off me.

By the light of the fire, the three Prims with him surveyed me. What did I look like to them? Blistered red by the sun, my own clothing ripped and dirty, a bloody gash on my knee, my short curly hair standing on end.

"The healer left this morning. Gone to collect supplies on the other side of the Mountain. When she returns, she can look at the wound. See what can be done."

"And until then?" Gideon asked.

Ezekiel went inside his hut and returned a moment later with a jar. "This paste will help. Rub it on the wound. Perhaps we can give her a few more days."

A few more days.

"She will need a place to sleep," Ezekiel pointed out.

"She can stay with me. I will sleep outside," Gideon added quickly.

Ezekiel nodded. "Sleep well," he said. Was it a touch of sarcasm in his voice?

Gideon nodded and bowed his head, respectfully. "Follow me," he said.

At one end of the camp, a cave mouth yawned wide and dark. A tower of stones, stacked to look like a body, sat outside guarding the entrance. "That's where you go if there's trouble," he told me. "And that's my shelter, over there." He pointed to a small hut. "It's just me, so it's small. But I can add on to it later, when I have a family." Gideon gave me a sidelong glance. I could feel his eyes running up and down my face. "Are you disappointed?"

I turned to him, not sure what he meant.

"In our camp. Is this what you thought it would be like?"

Up until yesterday, I hadn't given a Prim camp much thought. Even now, I was too overwhelmed to make sense of where I was. "It's dirty," I said. It was the first word that came to my mind. The clinical cleanliness of the City, the white light the City was bathed in, didn't exist here. "And dark."

"It looks different in daylight," Gideon said. He held open the door to his hut and stuck the torch in the ground outside. Firelight glowed through a square of glass. I could make out a small cot, a table and one chair. "It's simple, but it's home."

I took a step closer to the bed and stifled a scream. "What is that?" Lying on the bed was a mass of hair.

"What?" he asked.

"That!" I pointed.

"This? Fur. It keeps us warm."

I shuddered, disgusted.

"It's from animals we trap. We sew their hides together."

"I'd rather freeze than have that thing on me."

Gideon laughed. "You'll change your mind in winter."

There was an awkward moment as we both realized I wouldn't make it that long.

"I'll get you a different blanket and use the fur outside."

I nodded, weak with fatigue. As soon as Gideon pulled the fur from the bed, I collapsed on it. Ignoring the musky Prim odour, I shut my eyes and let sleep take me away.

Lev

Kaia was half-Prim? Was it possible?

Raf refused to let me rest, berating me if I slowed my pace. Maddeningly, he wouldn't tell me anything else about the experiment, claiming he didn't know. Could I believe him? In the back of my mind, I wondered if what he'd told me was a lie, some elaborate story invented by Tar.

"You're quiet," Raf said. He'd turned us back towards the stream after finding no more signs of Kaia deeper in the forest. He kept muttering that she couldn't be far. Twigs and branches snapped under our feet and unfamiliar bird calls filled the forest. My suit was muddy, dirt smudges covered the arms and legs. I'd taken off the face mask and pushed the hood back to hear and see better, no longer worried about exposure to the sun under the dense forest.

"I'm thinking."

"About Kaia," he guessed.

She was all I could think about. "Maybe she left because she found out."

Raf shook his head. "About being a half-breed? Doubt it. The information is secret, only the female who birthed her and a couple of overseers who were guarding the Prims knew. None of them would have told her."

"What about Sy? He must have known."

"The project leader knew what would happen if she told anyone."

I frowned at Raf's back as he walked ahead of me. "Kaia's birth elder died years ago," I said. "Kaia had never said how. Do you think—"

Raf held up his hand, cutting me off, and froze mid-step. A branch cracked in the forest. We waited for another noise, but when none came, we kept moving. I glanced over my shoulder. The feeling of being watched hadn't left me.

"It explains why Tar wouldn't let me match her," I said, more to myself than to Raf. But he made a noise of agreement in his throat anyway.

"And now you're out here, chasing her," he said, his voice a grim reminder of the irony.

"What will happen to Kaia when she's back in the City?"

Raf didn't answer right away. "They'll do experiments. Breed her. Harvest her blood for its antibodies, or whatever she has that makes her able to survive out here."

If she survived out here, I thought and a sick swell rose up my stomach.

"If we find her alive, she'll already have proven the most important thing: that interbreeding can make a better specimen."

"She's not a specimen. She's a Citizen," I muttered.

Raf stopped short and turned. "She's a half-breed."

I could have backed down. It wasn't worth arguing with him. He didn't know Kaia, but something about the disdain in his voice got my back up. "She was raised in the City. She has a pulse point."

He scoffed. "Her blood's not pure. That's why Tar wouldn't let you match with her."

"Yet, as you pointed out, we're out here searching for her."

"Only because we need her. We need to know what it is in their blood that makes them stronger than us," he growled.

"She is 'us'!" I yelled back.

Raf took a deep breath and closed his eyes, "Stay calm," he muttered. He opened his eyes and looked at me. "The hormone surges are making our tempers flare."

I glared at him, still angry. "The what?"

"In the City, our pulse points control our hormones. It's the only way to ensure we aren't ruled by emotions, keeps aggression to a minimum. Now that our connection with the City is broken, emotions are taking over. We're untethered. It explains the dizzy spells I'm getting. You're a bit younger than me. Maybe they won't affect you the same way."

I watched Raf hike a few paces ahead of me. He had disappeared into the trees and a minute later I was alone. Truly alone. What if I left Raf and followed another path? I could find Kaia, tell her the real reason we were tracking her. And then what? Make sure she never returned to the City? *No!* Prim blood or not, she belonged with me. I wasn't like Raf, repulsed by the idea of who her real birth elder was. How could I be? I'd known her my whole life. The truth about her progenitor didn't change how I felt about her.

But what if Raf was right? How could I bring her back knowing what lay in store for her?

Unless…I thought of Tar's desire for me to be a leader. As a leader, I could keep Kaia safe. The possibilities clashed against each other until my head spun.

Behind me, the trees rustled. That bird called again, its voice cutting through the silence, and a branch snapped. My heart pounded. What was I thinking? I couldn't survive out here. And neither could Kaia. "Raf!" I shouted. "Wait!" I barged through the trees until his white survival suit was within reach.

"Keep up," he grunted.

◦

The day had dragged on with no more clues. I kept my eyes on the ground along the stream hoping for a footprint, *something* to tell me we were on the right track. Raf had finally agreed to a break. We'd taken turns sleeping on the damp ground while the other one kept watch. He'd let me go first and I drifted off seconds after putting my head down, not caring about the cold that seeped through the suit or the stones that dug into my back.

But when it had been my turn to keep watch, I'd counted the seconds until I could wake Raf. I jumped at every noise. Sitting still left me vulnerable and too aware of the alien forest.

I regretted all the times I'd cursed the boredom of overseeing. What would I give to be back on the balcony, looking out over the gymnasium floor? My thoughts kept straying to Kaia. Where was she? Had it been Mae's balancing and my match with Sari that had pushed her to leave? Or something else? Had she learned the truth about who she was?

A growl deep in the forest made me nudge Raf awake with my foot. "Raf, get up." Raf's eyes flew open. He stretched and sat up, but looked as exhausted as he had before the nap.

"Already?" he groaned.

I didn't tell him that my rattled nerves had cheated him out of equal sleeping time. He stood, shaking out his limbs, and grabbed his canteen. He drained it and went to the stream. Squatting on his haunches, he filled the canteen with water and peered up and down the opposite shore. "The stream's narrow here. Maybe we should walk on the other side for a while." He didn't wait for me to reply as he crossed.

"I thought we'd have caught up to her by now," Raf said. I gritted my teeth in annoyance. It was the hundredth time he'd said that since we'd got to the Mountain. "We'll search until midday tomorrow. If we haven't found her by then, we'll have to go back."

"And leave her here?"

Raf set his mouth in a grim line and turned to me. Over the gurgle of the stream, he said, "Every minute we're on the Mountain puts us in danger. The Prims could have her hidden at one of their camps. Or maybe the beasts found her. We could be risking our lives searching for someone who's already dead."

I opened my mouth to argue but the words froze on my tongue. Behind him a pair of yellow eyes glowed from the bushes. "Raf!" I screamed. My warning came too late. Five beasts leapt out of the forest and surrounded Raf. They were enormous, shaggy-haired creatures, with humped backs and thick muscular hind legs. Raf crouched down, hands up, ready for combat as the animals circled him. One, the largest, bared his teeth, snarling. The others followed his lead.

I stayed where I was, watching, racking my brain for a way to help. Raf didn't look at me. His eyes were fixed on the biggest beast. The alpha flicked his head and a smaller beast leaped at Raf, knocking him to the ground. The others held their position, ears back, hackles raised, watching.

Raf kicked the beast off and rolled away, but it lunged at him again. This time, Raf pounded it on the snout. With a yelp, the animal backed off. The others jeered at him. Was that possible? That these beasts could laugh at each other? The attacker silenced them with a snarl and lunged again.

On the other side of the stream, I was ignored, all their energy was focused on Raf. They circled him, teeth gnashing, moving in closer. "My stick!" he yelled at me.

It was lying by his pack. I grabbed it and tossed it to him, but it landed on the ground too far to do any good. I picked up some rocks and hurled them at the animals' flanks, but missed. I ran closer, splashing through the shallow water. As soon as I was on the other side of the stream, the alpha turned and barked, his yellow eyes now trained on me. With a slow, menacing stalk, one of the other beasts came towards me, shoulder blades jutting out of its coat as it approached, and let out a low, bone-chilling growl.

"Raf!" I yelled. I threw a rock, but my hands shook and I missed. The animal's eyes narrowed, teeth bared. A trickle of warm pee ran down my leg.

I looked at Raf. He kicked at a beast and dove for the walking stick, dragging it to him. Swinging his weapon, he kept his back to the stream and walked towards me. Each time a beast got close, he whacked it. The beasts were growing frustrated, their snarls more harried. "Raf!" I yelled again. I was defenceless. Stupidly,

I'd left my knife in my pack and I didn't have a stick to swing at them. Raf kicked at one of his attackers, making contact with its soft underbelly. The animal yelped and Raf kicked it again, so hard it flew backwards, and then it scampered up and hobbled into the trees.

Before the alpha could bark another command, Raf went after him, the walking stick spinning like a wind turbine, and he hit it on the snout, then kicked its jaw. The stunned animal retreated, slinking down towards the forest but never taking its eyes off Raf.

The beast coming for me slunk closer, a low growl deep in its belly. When it opened its mouth to bark, I jumped. I could taste my fear, cloying and bitter, it rose off me like a stink. I scrambled across the stream, trying to get to my feet before it came at me. But it stayed where it was, like the stream was an invisible wall.

A spear cut through the air and hit the animal. With a shriek of pain, it spun around. Raf's walking stick was lodged in its hind-quarters. Raf raised his arms and let loose a deep, primal scream. He stomped through the water, ripped the walking stick out of the wounded creature, and beat it. The animal howled in pain and fell on its side. The alpha barked and the others retreated to the forest, scurrying through the underbrush.

Raf gripped the walking stick in both hands, raised it above his head and plunged it deep into the animal's neck. A gurgle of blood spilled from its mouth. It spasmed once. Twice. And then lay still. My breath came in short bursts and I started trembling. "Is it dead?" I could smell my own piss.

Raf yanked the stick out of the animal. The pointed end was covered in blood. He wiped the blood on his fingers and rubbed them together, then smeared it across his cheeks. I watched him, horrified. He held his stick up in ready position and peered across the stream into the forest. There was no movement. "This one is."

I pointed to a rip in his suit. "Are you hurt?"

He glanced at it, pulling the fabric closer for inspection. "Didn't puncture the skin. These suits are tough. We better keep moving. They've got our scent now. They'll be back."

Panic rose in me at the thought of being tracked. What if the pack grew? What if next time, it was ten against two?

"They wanted to kill us."

"They want us off their Mountain. I told you they were territorial."

I grabbed my pack with shaking hands. If they came back, the knife I'd brought wouldn't suffice. I needed something ready, something that could bludgeon. I grabbed a branch from the ground. It was heavy, the diameter of my calf and as long as my forearm. Strips of wet bark peeled off the sides, uncovering the wood underneath. As I took a few practice swings, I felt the weight of it rip through the air. If those beasts came at me again, I'd be ready.

Raf grunted his approval and started walking. I gripped the club in my hand and a thought flickered in my mind. The club wasn't just a weapon against a beast; a blow across the back of the head could kill a man too.

Kaia

"You let her sleep in your hut?" A female's shout woke me. I didn't know how long I'd been sleeping, but when I tried to sit up, my back and legs were so stiff, I groaned. I pulled back the covers and lifted the bandage to look at my throbbing knee. I was relieved to see infection hadn't spread. The poultice must have helped.

I stood up and hobbled to the door.

Outside, the red-haired Prim named Nadia stood glaring at Gideon as he sat on a stone, calmly tending to a small fire. "Where should I have let her sleep? In the garden?"

"She could have slit your neck in the night," Nadia hissed.

I cleared my throat and pushed the door open further. It was at least midday, the sun was high overhead. The girl stared and I stared back. "I couldn't slit his neck," I said, wryly. "He has my knife."

Gideon shot me a look. "That'll put her mind at ease."

I turned to Nadia, noticing how her skin was covered with speckles, like a bird's egg. In the sun, her hair glinted a fiery orange. "I didn't escape the City to hurt you."

It took her a second to find her voice. "You could be a spy and the rest of them are waiting in the forest to attack."

With an exasperated sigh, I turned to Gideon. "Tell her how you dragged me into a cave."

"It's true," he admitted. "We didn't give her much choice."

"Much choice," I snorted. "*No* choice."

She narrowed her eyes at me. "I thought you were weak and injured. You look fine to me."

I held up the hem of my tunic so she could see the bandage. "Well, I'm not. And from what Akrum said, I'm just waiting to die anyway, so you won't have to worry about me coming after Gideon, or anyone else, in their sleep."

She looked at Gideon with an arched eyebrow as if he was the traitor and marched off.

"Are all Prims so welcoming?"

"You're in a fine mood," he said.

I gave an exasperated sigh. "The woman I came to find is dead. I've been accused of being a murderer. The cut on my knee will likely kill me and the person who could help me, your healer, is gone till nobody knows when. What kind of a mood should I be in?"

Gideon didn't reply. Instead, he reached for a shiny pot and a cup. "Tea?"

I sat in a huff across the fire. "I'm also cold."

"One of the elders, Josephina, brought you some clothes. They're on the chair inside."

I went back into the hut and found them, folded neatly. Goosebumps prickled across my skin as I took off my ripped, mud-spattered tunic and put on a pair of pants and a roughly woven shirt that billowed around my arms and torso. The pants were an unaccustomed weight, but warm. There was also a cloak made of dead animals like the thing Gideon had had on his bed. I turned away at its unfamiliar, tangy odour.

"Warmer?" Gideon asked when I joined him outside. He passed me a cup of tea.

"It was kind of her," I said. "To bring me the clothes. And nice to know they don't all think I'm going to kill you in your sleep."

"It's not Nadia's fault she doesn't trust you."

"She doesn't even know me."

"She knows you're from the City. That's enough."

I blew on the tea to cool it. Tea in the City was drunk cold. I guess on the Mountain any source of heat was welcome. I thought it was a waste of energy to heat a drink, but didn't say anything to Gideon. "I still don't understand why they hate me."

"You don't?"

"No." I bristled at his reaction. "You're the ones who want to attack the City. Maybe not lately, but—"

Gideon shook his head. "That's not true, Kaia. We want nothing to do with the City. We know what really goes on there. We know what your people want to do to us."

"What are you talking about?"

"The underland. We know what goes on there."

I gaped at him. I didn't even know what went on in the underland. "How could you know?"

He gave me a long look, his face serious.

"What is it? I pressed. "What do you know about my city that I don't?"

Gideon shook his head again. "It's not for me to tell you. Now that you're rested, my grandfather can explain it. He asked me to bring you to him when you woke up."

"Who's your grandfather?"

"Chief Ezekiel."

I heard the pride in his voice.

As grouchy as I'd been to him, I realized that he was my only friend on the Mountain. The thought of being in anyone's company besides Gideon's made me nervous. "Will you stay with me?" I asked.

"Yes, if you want me to."

The hot tea melted away some of the chill. Gideon entertained me with stories of the annual solstice party they held for the longest day of the year and how the whole camp celebrated when hunters returned with fresh meat. It sounded disgusting to eat an animal, but I hid my revulsion. He explained that at their celebrations there was dancing and singing, two things that weren't done in the City. "You make it sound like it's a happy place," I said.

He gave me a funny look. "It is."

He wasn't telling me about the dangers though. Or the rough living conditions. I knew those things existed too. How could anyone think they were truly in a happy place when safety was always a concern?

As soon as I'd drained my second cup of tea, Gideon stood. "We shouldn't keep the Chief waiting. Ready?"

I didn't think 'no' was an option, so I put my cup on the ground and followed him. My stomach dropped when I realized we'd have to walk right through the camp to get to Ezekiel's hut.

In the daylight, the Prim camp didn't look as gloomy as it had when I'd arrived. The men all looked like Gideon, with beards, muscular bodies and broad shoulders. Together, they were an intimidating group, hairy and wild-looking with weathered skin.

I tried to ignore their suspicious looks and the occasional hiss. I guessed that since Gideon was still breathing, they assumed I wasn't a murderous villain. They were clearly talking about me and had no shame in staring me up and down as I walked towards Ezekiel's shelter.

If they could stare at me, I'd stare right back, I decided. I noticed the women walked with a side-to-side gait, their backs bent from years of hard work, long braids swinging over their shoulders. The ones of child-bearing age had soft curves discernible even through their loose clothing. One, sitting by the fire, stared at me with naked curiosity. Her long hair, bleached blond and matted, reminded me of a filthy, unkempt version of Sari.

I'd been expecting to go to the same hut I'd seen Ezekiel at the night before, but instead Gideon led me to the largest shelter in the camp. Metal siding and dome-shaped windows covered one side of it and layers of other materials had been stacked haphazard. A trail of smoke coiled into the sky through a hole in the roof.

Suddenly the door opened and a male walked out, prodded forward by Akrum, who carried a long stick. The male's hands were bound and his head hung down. As he walked towards the centre of camp, people stopped their work and stood still, hissing. Anyone inside a shelter came outside glaring at the male, teeth bared in an angry jeer. Akrum egged the crowd on, lifting his arms until the cries of derision were deafening.

I turned to Gideon, panicked.

"He's been accused of something. And found guilty by the looks of it." He was unconcerned by the raucous calls and spitting of the other Prims.

Akrum raised the stick above his head. The noise stopped. Ezekiel walked past me, hobbling on bowed legs, and stood beside Akrum and the male. "Rufus," his voice rang out, "you have been found guilty of stealing from another camp and sentenced to public shaming and twenty lashes."

The male closed his eyes and took a shaky inhalation.

"On your hands and knees," Akrum said. The man bent down. I looked to Gideon with alarm. "What is he going to do?"

"Twenty lashes," Gideon said simply. "His punishment for stealing."

I'd never seen harm inflicted this way. I turned away, horrified. "Why do you do that?"

"It's how we teach right from wrong. You see," Gideon pointed to a group of children. Their elders stood beside them. The children's wide eyes were glued to the stick in Akrum's hand. "They must see what happens to those who disobey the rules of our camp."

Akrum's stick came down hard across Rufus's back. I winced as the slap of the stick on flesh echoed in the silent camp. Rufus arched his back and gasped, but the next blow came quickly and the one after that, quicker. Rufus's arms shook with effort, his face contorted with pain. When the final five blows were to be delivered, the Prims began a countdown. "Five," they shouted out, "Four," their voices rang loud in the camp, "Three," there was excitement, "Two," Akrum paused and looked at Rufus's chewed-up back with satisfaction, "One!" a feverish glee followed. Rufus collapsed on the ground, his back covered in red welts, some wounds open and raw.

"You have been punished. The crime is forgotten and will not be mentioned." Akrum spun around to take in the many faces watching. "Agreed?" he called out.

"Agreed!" The Prims responded and then began clapping, as if it was a celebration.

Akrum held out a hand to Rufus. "It is done," he said. The man staggered to his feet, leaning on Akrum. A female and two young children ran to Rufus. His family, I assumed. The boys had stood watching, perhaps even counting, while Akrum had delivered the blows.

The rest of the camp returned to their work as the woman led Rufus to his shelter. I looked at Gideon. "That was horrible!" I sputtered.

"This is how things are done."

"They beat him! He could barely stand!"

Gideon tugged on my arm and pulled me aside. "It seems inhumane to you?" he asked.

I nodded.

"So what do they do in the City?"

"I…I," I stammered to answer him. The truth was, I didn't know.

"If someone needs to be punished, we all see it."

Rufus and his family had left the clearing, but Ezekiel was still there, playing a game with some children. They laid their palms on his and he tried to slap their hands before they could pull them away. The children shrieked and giggled, clamouring for a turn.

Rufus's beating was already forgotten as parents laughed at their children who jumped up and down desperate to be next in line to play the game. Other adults had gone back to their work, cooking or tending to the fire. A female sang as she hung clothes to dry.

I had to admit, the Prims seemed content. There was laughter and happy chatter. "I guess we seem primitive to you? Living up to our name?" Gideon's tone was light, as if he didn't believe it anyway.

I frowned. "I didn't know what to expect, to be honest. I left the City so quickly, all I thought about was getting away, but not about where I was going."

"Will you tell me now? About why you left?"

Ezekiel tousled the hair of one child and waved goodbye to them, moving towards the hut. He gestured for Gideon and me to join him. Other elders who had come out to watch Rufus's punishment followed. Gideon and I stood to the side while Akrum, Ezekiel, and three others sat in a semi-circle on the other side of the small fire. I recoiled when I saw what hung above them: a bird, its wings stretched, the feathers dull and oily. Not as big as the one that had tried to attack me, but still creepy.

"It's not real," Gideon whispered. "My great-grandfather followed a raven to this spot and that is why we settled here."

"So he killed it?" I whispered back.

Gideon shrugged. "He wanted to keep the luck around us."

A fire crackled in the middle of the shelter. Even with the hole in the ceiling, the air was thick with smoke and my eyes burned because of it. Ezekiel gestured for us to sit and fixed me with a penetrating gaze.

Finally, he spoke. "So, Kaia, tell us why you have come."

"I came," the words stuck in my throat, "to find my birth elder. My mother."

They exchanged looks.

"Her name was Raina. She left the City sixteen years ago."

Ezekiel peered at me. "And your father?"

"He stayed behind with me. Raina left alone."

He shook his head. "We have no Raina here."

The hope that Akrum had been lying to me or keeping Raina's whereabouts a secret was dashed.

"Since I have been Chief, we have had five refugees. All but one died. She is our healer, but her name is not Raina and she did not leave alone."

A great pressure built up in my chest. What was I going to do? Stay here with these people, these *Prims?* Or try to return to the City and face whatever punishment awaited me.

Ezekiel scuttled over to me and sat so close I could see his nose hairs quiver when he breathed. I leaned away, but he grabbed my hand in his and examined my pulse point. "You know this must be removed."

"I told you, it's broken."

"How can you be sure? How can we be sure?"

I could tell him about the overseers in the valley. They'd have found me by now if the pulse point was still connected to the City. But telling him I'd been followed wouldn't build any trust. It would do the opposite.

But Raina wasn't here, which meant I had no reason to stay with the Prims. I could go back. And then what? How would I explain my absence? Or a missing pulse point?

"How can I be sure you won't try to kill me?" I fired back.

Ezekiel's face split into a grin, his yellow, rotted teeth exposed. "You can't."

"Looks like we both have to trust each other." I held Ezekiel's gaze for a long moment. "What about infection? It can't be safe to remove the pulse point without your healer."

"We can wait for the healer to return," the female elder said. The others nodded in agreement.

Ezekiel dropped my hand. I clutched it to my chest, grateful it would stay intact for a while longer. Or maybe forever. I could leave their camp, go back to the City and beg forgiveness. Tell the overseers that grief had made me act crazy. I could make up a story about wandering the Mountain until I came to my senses.

"Tell me, Kaia," Ezekiel said, "What do you know of us?"

I hesitated. The truth would offend him, but anything less and he might distrust me. "You live a simple life. Primitive. Genetics don't matter here."

Ezekiel took a deep breath and rocked back on his feet. "No," he said, shaking his head. "That's where you're wrong. How could all of us have survived out here unless genetics *did* matter?" He gestured at the female elder. "You see Josephina? Her sister died young. Barely made it out of childhood. But Josephina, she has already lived a long life, eh? Why is that?" Ezekiel looked at me with wild eyes. "Do you know?"

I shook my head.

"Bah!" he swatted at me, exhaling rancid breath in my face. "Of course you don't. None of you do." Ezekiel clapped the tips of his fingers together and bounced on his toes. He reminded me of Sy during one of his manic episodes, the ones where Mae and I would squeeze into her sleeping capsule and wait for it to be over. "She doesn't know," he muttered. "Why doesn't she know?"

A male elder spoke up. "She doesn't know because they don't want anyone to know."

"Yes!" Ezekiel hissed. "Your City is built on lies! You are taught to fear us, that we are dangerous. That we live a miserable existence on the Mountain. Tell me, Kaia, do we seem miserable to you?" He didn't wait for me to answer. "It is your people who are not to be trusted. Once we asked for help and the City betrayed us."

I looked at Gideon, but his eyes were trained on his grandfather.

"Tell her, Zacharias. Tell her what the City wants to keep secret."

One of the elders began to speak. He had a deep voice and spoke slowly, as if each word carried great weight. "A horrible illness came to the Mountain. We feared we would all die, women, children, our fiercest hunters. It was decided that our two strongest men would trek to the City. They would ask for help, medicines or supplies. Winter was upon us and we worried that our entire people would be wiped out. We sent them down and waited for days and then weeks. It was a long, cruel winter and when spring came, we were half of who we'd been. The men never returned. We came to find out later that not only had the City refused to help us, but they had captured these men, holding them in underground chambers as prisoners."

I gaped at the elder in disbelief. There were no Prims in the City. "How do you know this?"

This time, it was Ezekiel who answered. "The question is, how do you *not* know this? Your City is full of secrets, Kaia. You are taught to fear us, but perhaps the real danger lies inside the dome, not outside."

At his words, even the warmth of the fire couldn't drive out the chill that ran up my spine.

Lev

The adrenaline rush of the attack kept me alert as we moved further up the Mountain. For the rest of the day my eyes darted around at the slightest sound in the trees looking for a flash of fur. I was surprised when Raf stopped before night had fallen. "We need to make camp." He stabbed his walking stick into the ground and leaned on it. The animal's blood on his cheek had dried, fading to brown.

I nodded in agreement, relieved. "Not on the ground," I muttered. Since the beasts had attacked, I'd started to feel the effects of being untethered. I didn't get dizzy like Raf, but my moods swung between euphoria and a raging anger. Each rolled through me, confusingly quick. "The surges," I muttered. "They're giving me a headache."

"Me too. And we're dehydrated. We need to rest." Raf's eyes swept the forest and landed on a slab of rock on the other side of the stream. Not part of the Mountain, it looked as though it had tumbled down from the peak and this was where it had landed.

"How do we get up there?"

Raf pointed to where a tree trunk had fallen, making a ramp to the top over the stream.

"We can climb it," he said. He didn't ask my opinion. An unreasonable rush of anger filled me. I pushed it away, reminding myself it was the hormone surges. I kept myself in check. His footsteps were deft and sure, and seconds later, he was standing on top of the stone, surveying the forest beneath him. "Throw me your pack," he shouted. I hurled it up, took a deep breath and began the climb. I wanted to go on all fours and crawl, but Raf was watching, appraising. Holding my arms out to balance myself, I concentrated on placing each foot carefully. Beads of perspiration popped out on my forehead and I wondered how he'd done it so effortlessly.

"Don't look down," Raf called to me.

Too nervous to nod, I kept walking. My palms were sweaty. I paused to steady my footing and saw the ground below. The stream passed under me, but the bed was shallow and littered with sticks and stones. A tumble off the tree would be a disaster. Taking a steadying breath, I looked at Raf. He was close, no more than an arm's length or two away.

My breath quickened. I was almost there.

"You can do it," Raf said, holding out his hand.

A sudden burst of movement caught me off guard. A swarm of small birds exploded from the trees to my right. Hundreds of them filled the sky, swooping down and skimming the top of my head. I ducked and wobbled on the tree trunk. "Raf!" I shouted and spun my arms, but there was nothing to hold on to. I felt myself falling.

Raf lunged, catching my arm. "I got you!" My legs slipped out from under me so my bottom half was hanging off the tree trunk. "Swing your leg up."

"I can't!" Fear left me paralyzed.

"You have to!" Raf tugged on my arm. "You're slipping, Lev."

It was true. He was losing his grip on the survival suit. With a grunt of effort and a strength I didn't know I had, I swung one leg up. My toes touched the trunk but fell off. "I'm going to fall!"

Raf adjusted his grip, leaning further off the rock. If I fell, we were both going down. I hauled my torso further up and then hooked my heel around the tree.

"That's it," Raf encouraged.

I inched myself closer to the rock until my chin was resting on it. Raf yanked me the rest of the way and I landed in a heap. I wanted to laugh with relief and cry in frustration. How many more brushes with death would we have before we found Kaia?

If we found Kaia.

Kaia

Ezekiel had nodded for me to leave the elder's meeting place after his revelation about the City. Had he wanted to shock me? Or was he sincere that I know the truth? I barely registered the looks the Prims gave me as Gideon escorted me through the clearing. "I can't believe the City would do that," I said shaking my head. "It's so," I tried to think of the right word. "Savage."

Gideon looked at me thoughtfully. "We've heard about balancings, where you kill the old and weak."

"But that's because they don't produce energy. A city can't run if its own Citizens can't support it."

Gideon stopped walking and held on to my elbow. "We help each other. We survive."

"It's different here," I replied.

"How?"

"Because you're—" The word 'desperate' was on the tip of my

tongue, but that was a lie. No one here looked desperate. They lived simply, but that wasn't the same. None of the Prims had expressed any interest in going to the City. To them, we were the ones to be pitied.

"Gideon?" a boy from across the clearing called. "Is that you?" He walked tentatively with a stick in front of him, tapping it on stones embedded in the ground. I hadn't noticed before, but they ran all over the Prim camp. The boy came closer and I saw he was older than I thought, maybe fifteen or sixteen. His skin was burnished a deep brown and his hair was streaked with blond. He was lean and almost my height, but would grow taller; I saw how his neck had already stretched and was waiting for the rest of his body to catch up and fill out.

He stared straight past me, like I wasn't there. One eye was cloudy green, as if the white had bled into the colour, and the other was a marled, brownish colour, fixated on something in the distance.

"What's wrong with him?" I whispered to Gideon.

"He's blind."

I took a step back, revolted. "A defective."

Gideon shook his head. "No, just blind."

"I've never seen one before." But I'd heard of anomalies in my training. We'd done our best to eradicate weaknesses like his from our genetics. I thought of the female I'd lied to about her fetus. What if he was born like this Prim? The City would balance the infant—and with good reason. A sudden flash of regret filled me. I shouldn't have been so soft with her. The truth would come out eventually and then she'd have to deal with the consequences.

"It's me, Sepp. Over here. Take the path to the left."

Sepp's stick tapped, looking for the stone path that would lead him to us.

I moved away, behind Gideon, but he pulled me forward. "I want you to meet Kaia."

"The girl from the City? I heard about her."

"She's never seen a blind person before. I think she's a little nervous."

Sepp smiled. "I won't bite. At least, I don't usually."

At first, I looked away, not wanting to see him face to face. But then I remembered he couldn't see me. I stared at him unabashedly, getting an eyeful.

"Does she talk?" Sepp asked.

"Y-yes," I stammered. "I talk."

"Good!" Sepp sounded happy. How could he be though? Living a life without eyes? What kind of a cruel progenitor would want this life for their offspring?

"So your mother's back too?" Gideon asked. "Kaia has a wound on her knee that we need her to look at."

"He belongs to the healer?" I asked incredulous.

"Yes." Sepp turned his head in my direction. It was unsettling the way they looked through me.

"Is she at home?" Gideon asked.

"She was when I left. I'm going to check the garden. I'll see you later."

Gideon guided him towards a different path. I turned to watch him go. A group of children yelled greetings to him.

"It's like he's one of you," I said when Gideon came back to me.

"He is one of us."

"I know, I mean you accept him as one of you."

Gideon took a deep, irritated breath. "You're going to have to let go of your City ideas. He's not contagious, he's blind. You should see the carvings he does. They're incredible."

Gideon pulled at a thin cord under his shirt. "Sepp made this for me."

Intricately carved, it was the face of the bird that had hung over Ezekiel.

"It's a whistle. We all have them. It's how we let others know if there's danger." He put the whistle to his lips and blew gently. A high-pitched noise pierced the air. I had to admit, I was impressed. "The sound stuns beasts too," he said.

"The beasts? They're real?"

"They roam the north side of the Mountain. They're vicious," he said warningly, "and travel in packs. As long as you don't cross the stream, they'll leave you alone. If the healer's back, we should go to her."

"So she can look at my knee?" It felt hot to the touch, but it didn't look any worse.

"And," he gave my finger a meaningful look. "My grandfather's right. It has to come out."

"How?"

Gideon took my hand and held it palm up. "The healer will make an incision here," he drew a line along my fingertip. It sent a shiver up my arm. "And take it out. I'm sure it will hurt, but if you survive the wound on your knee..." He shrugged and I pulled my hand away.

I tucked my arms around my body.

"No one's forcing you to. You could go back to the City," he said.

His mention of the City reminded me that I wasn't the only Citizen on the Mountain. *The overseers.* Were they still looking for me? Or had they gone back to the City. Why had they even come? Sy wouldn't have told them about my escape—not willingly. With a start, I realized that they could have found him returning from the underland alone and questioned him. If he'd been forced to admit the truth, the overseers might have come after me.

Oh, Sy, I thought with regret. *What have you done?*

If Raina had been here, like Sy believed, things would have been different. I would have had a reason to stay, but as it was, I was trapped in a place I didn't belong, with a people I didn't understand.

Lev

I squeezed my eyes shut and groaned. "I hate it out here!" I was still trembling from my failed climb up the tree trunk. The muscles in my torso and arms ached.

"I know," Raf said. "But you're doing good. Tar would be proud." He slapped me on the back.

I clenched my teeth. "I don't care about Tar." It was her fault we were out here. Partially, anyway.

"No?"

"No."

He eyed me, but said nothing. He shoved my pack at me. "We should eat. Try to gain some strength." I pulled out a rice cake and cold, mushy beans. My food supply was dwindling.

"We'll head back tomorrow at midday," Raf reminded me licking his fingers clean. I'd lost my appetite and put the food back in my pack. "You can sleep first and I'll keep watch. I'll wake you in a couple of hours. We can start moving again when it's light out."

The last wisps of daylight disappeared as I lay my head on a mossy patch of rock.

Our second night outside and my thoughts drifted to Kaia. Closing my eyes, I conjured the memory of us in the orchard. Without my pulse point to help, it was hard, but eventually the feel of her, the taste of her lips came back to me. A longing filled me that I'd never experienced; the urgency of it made me blush.

Raf was following orders. He was determined to hunt Kaia and bring her back to the City, just as Tar had commanded. But I wasn't out here because of Tar's orders. I was looking for Kaia because I couldn't imagine living without her. I knew what I had to do. Searching the Mountain could take days, weeks maybe. Raf would never agree to let me go on my own. The only way I could keep looking for Kaia was if I slipped away while Raf slept. By the time he woke up and realized I was gone, I'd be too far away for him to catch.

Kaia

Two huts stood in front of us. Gideon walked towards the larger one. It had a stone base and thatched roof, bits of sticks and bones dangled on strings from the trees, tinkling as we walked past. Baskets of plants, some with the roots still attached, lay by the door.

"Healer?" Gideon called softly, rapping on the door.

"Come in," a voice called.

Gideon pushed the door open. The room was dim, a few tapered candles flickered on the mud-packed floor. Dried plants tied with string hung from the rafters and filled the air with spicy, herbal aromas. A woman bent over a stone bowl, pounding the leaves inside into a fine powder. One thick braid hung down, hiding her face. She was so intent on her work, she didn't look up when we entered. Gideon cleared his throat.

"Gideon," she said with a smile, standing up. Her skin was ruddy and drawn, like the other Prims.

"You heard about the refugee?"

Her eyes flickered to me, warily. "Yes. Hello," she said. "I was just making a fresh dressing for your wound."

I stared at her mutely.

"Sit," she gestured to the cot, bigger than Gideon's and piled with extra blankets. "How was the journey? Besides your knee, were there any other injuries?"

"My skin still hurts from the sun and I have insect bites."

The candle light made shadows flicker across her face. As she came closer, I couldn't take my eyes off her. My heart thumped in my chest.

"What's your name?" she asked.

My mouth went dry. "Kaia," I whispered. I knew her face.

The stone bowl crashed to the floor and the healer rushed to my side. Her hands shook as she peered into my face. "Kaia?"

When her eyes travelled over my face, a connection, lost long ago, rekindled. A spark lit. My skin prickled.

"Kaia," my name, so familiar on her tongue, wrapped me in its long-forgotten sound. From somewhere deep in the recesses of my mind, her voice found its way forward. "Is it really you?"

Her hands flew to her face, covering her mouth. She shook her head, as if she couldn't believe it was true. I nodded. Unable to speak.

With trembling fingers, she stroked my cheeks, my hair and reached down for my hands, clasping them to her chest and drinking in every feature of my face. "Oh, Kaia," she gasped and held me like she never wanted to let go.

And then her sobs turned to laughter. "Go!" she said to Gideon. "Tell Ezekiel my daughter has found us!"

Lev

"Lev!" Raf shook me awake. I rubbed the sleep out of my eyes wondering how a few hours could feel like only minutes. "Your turn." He held his lightstick out for me. Reluctantly, I took it. My mouth was dry and I felt like I could have slept for days. I watched jealously as Raf collapsed on the other side of the rock and was snoring within seconds.

I tried to stay alert listening to the sounds of the forest. I'd planned on leaving when the first streaks of light appeared in the sky, but I was too antsy. I shook my canteen. Half full. I stood up and grabbed the branch I'd been carrying as a weapon. Standing over Raf, I realized how easy it would be to clobber him with it while he slept.

I shook my head, frustrated at the thoughts that kept entering my brain. I wasn't thinking clearly. I couldn't hurt Raf—he'd saved my life. Twice. But if he was hurt, it would be easier to escape him. I could take as long as I wanted to find Kaia.

I reminded myself that he wanted to bring Kaia back to the City to keep her as a prisoner. He thought she was less than him, a half-breed. The competing thoughts crowded my brain. Finally, I put his lightstick beside him and left him there.

I was halfway down the tree trunk when I heard a noise in the trees behind me. A rustling and snapping of twigs. I froze and listened harder.

"What was that?" Raf sat up, instantly alert. His body taut. He hadn't been sleeping as soundly as I thought. He reached for the lightstick. As soon as he held it, it glowed.

Breath caught in my throat as I waited for him to realize I was running away. The noises in the bush sounded again. Was it the beasts? Or Prims? "What are you doing?" he whispered, frowning. The beam of the lightstick made me squint as he shone it my way. He'd notice my pack and a guilty flush that crept up my neck. "You were leaving."

My heart hammered my guilt, but I shook my head. "No. I'm thirsty. I needed water."

"Why are you wearing your pack?" He narrowed his eyes at me, reaching slowly for his knife.

"I didn't want to leave it." There was another rustle in the trees. We both turned. "There's something out there." I scrambled back up the tree to the rock, not caring how clumsy I looked.

We both stood poised for movement, but the sounds stopped. "Where were you really going?" he asked.

"I told you. To get water."

"No, there's more going on." He looked at me suspiciously. "You're fidgeting. What are you hiding? Did you see her? Was that the noise in the bushes?" By the glow of the lightstick, I could see his eyes were round and agitated. He was having another spell. "Tar warned me this might happen. She said you were too much like Kellan."

I felt a surge of anger and tried to squash it. "Kellan was a hero," I said. "He died for the City."

Raf sneered. "That's what you were told. There's a lot you don't know."

"About Kellan?"

"About what it takes to be an overseer." He narrowed his eyes in a challenge. "About doing what the City needs you to. Kellan let his feelings affect his work. He couldn't be trusted. We gave him a choice. The Prims or the City."

I shook my head, not believing him. "He fell from the conductor. Citizens saw it happen."

"Yes. An 'accident.'" Raf didn't bother to hide his real meaning.

"You killed him?"

"It had to be done." I waited for a flash of regret, but all I saw was triumph. "He thought holding the Prims captive was cruel. He wanted us to release them. Kellan turned out to be a traitor to the City."

"You're lying. This is another trick." A hot pulse of anger rolled through me. I fought to keep it at bay. I needed to stay clear-headed.

He smirked, "Kellan wasn't a hero. He was weak. Just like you."

I ran at him. I didn't care that he had a knife or was stronger than me. None of it mattered when I threw my full weight against him. With a shout of surprise and a groan, he hit the rock. The knife clattered out of his hand. I reached for it, but he grabbed me in a headlock. His arm squeezed my windpipe. I was choking and gasping, blackness crept into the corners of my eyes. One arm loosened as he reached the knife. I spun out of his grip. Free, but weaponless.

"Don't make the same mistake Kellan did. This is your chance to prove yourself. A Prim's life isn't worth a Citizen's."

"She's *not* a Prim," I fired back angrily.

"She's a half-breed. Useful, yes, but not an equal."

Through Raf's words, I heard Tar's voice, her whispered plans filling him with hope for power. Kellan had seen through them and been killed for it. I'd stupidly volunteered to be a pawn in her game of manipulation. My naivety was no match for Tar's wickedness. Or Raf's.

From the corner of my eye, I saw a movement in the bushes. "Raf," I said, dropping my voice to a whisper. "They're here." His eyes widened and he turned to look. In that second, I kicked him between the legs and he went down, moaning in pain and grabbing himself. The knife clanged against the rock.

I picked up the knife. *I should kill him.* It's what he did to Kellan. He got to his feet and raised his hands in defeat. I moved closer to him, the knife's point aimed at his throat. There was no mistaking my intent. He walked backwards, keeping one eye on me and one on the edge of the boulder.

"You're not yourself," he said. "You're untethered, the surges are controlling you. Put the knife down so we can talk about this. I wasn't going to hurt you. I was never going to hurt you. I needed you to know the truth."

He was desperate now that I had the upper hand. "You killed him. You'd kill me too, if you could." Had that been Tar's order? The real reason she let me leave the City with him? My stomach rolled at the thought. I concentrated on keeping the knife steady as another surge hit me.

"Before you do something you'll regret, you need to know something. It's not just us that are outside. Tar was going to release a team of overseers every forty-eight hours until Kaia was found. If it's not us who find her, someone else will."

I narrowed my eyes at him. "You're trying to trick me."

He shook his head. "And when they find out what you've done to me, your days are numbered."

My breath came in fast bursts.

"It's for the good of the City, Lev." His tongue dripped with sarcasm and a hot flush rose up my neck. It spilled into my head with a roar.

I lunged at him. He took a step backwards, dodging the knife, but misjudged his footing. His arms windmilled in an effort to right himself. I was close enough to save him, like he'd done for me last night.

But I didn't reach out, instead I gave him a swift kick to his kneecap. A second later, he had tumbled over the side of the rock, falling from such a height that when he landed, it was in a motionless heap on the ground.

I stared in shock at Raf's body. One leg stuck out at an odd angle, the bone probably broken. I started to sweat. Remorse coursed through me, hot and sticky, it glued itself to my throat and made it hard to swallow. "Raf!"

He moaned and tried to roll over but cried out in pain and reached for his leg. Movement behind a tree caught my eye. A beast, crouched low, growled, then crept closer.

"Raf!" I cried, though I knew it was pointless. Hearing my

scream made the beast jump into action. It darted to Raf. "No! Please, no!" In a flash, it went at him, biting and ripping. Tearing his suit and digging into his exposed flesh. Raf's shrieks echoed off the rock.

I pulled my knees up to my chest, squeezed my eyes shut and covered my ears. Rocking on the boulder, I tried to shut out Raf's screams. My stomach heaved as I thought about what the beast was doing to him. I curled up on the rock, shivering, wishing for it to end. Finally, it was silent except for the sound of the beast gnawing and licking the flesh off Raf's bones.

Were there others lying in wait? Why had this one come alone? Raf had said they were intelligent and protective. A chilling thought ran up my spine. Were the beasts vengeful too? Had this one attacked in revenge for the one Raf had killed?

The beast looked over, twisting its mangy head. The long pink tongue lapped its snout clean of Raf's remains, as if to say, "I'm done here." With a yawn, it stretched its back, threw me one more look and loped into the forest.

Kaia

Raina and I had been sitting on the cot in her shelter reliving our lives for hours. Candles, long tapers of wax, had shrunk to nubs, dripping puddles of wax on the floor.

She wanted to know everything and my mouth had gone dry from the telling. Mae's balancing had been the hardest to explain. She'd held herself as if she was breaking apart, rocking gently for all that had been lost.

"What about Sy?" she asked, tentative, wiping her eyes with the heel of her hand. I frowned. Mixed-up feelings for him swirled in my head. I didn't know which ones would break free first. "Is he still alive?" she asked.

I nodded. "It was his idea for me to leave. I thought he was coming too," my voice broke. "He said to tell you he was sorry. And that he wished he was as brave as you."

"Oh, Sy," she said, her voice heavy with regret. "He bought you time," she said gently. "If your escape had been noticed," her voice trailed off. "He's always protected you." Her eyes, so much like Mae's it was unnerving, searched mine for understanding.

I shook my head. "Protected me? He sent me to die out here." I looked at my knee. Raina had spread a lumpy paste on the wound and wrapped it with a bandage. The shock of finding Raina alive had kept my feelings of bitterness at bay, but now they surged forward. "I never should have trusted Sy."

"You aren't going to die, Kaia."

"But Akrum said—"

"He didn't know you were my daughter."

Hearing her use the word 'daughter' made the breath catch in my throat. Raina reached out a tentative hand and shuffled closer to me on the cot.

"I asked for you as soon as I got here. But no one knew who you were."

Raina shook her head. "I'm called Mara here. I was worried overseers would come after me so I lied. I told the Prims my mate and I had left with our daughter, but only I had survived."

"And Sepp?"

Raina, Mara, I corrected myself, raised her eyebrows in surprise. "How did you—?"

"I met him. So it's true? That defective—"

"We don't use that word here," she cut me off, repeating Gideon's sentiments. She took my hands in hers. They were warm and strong. "He's blind," she said matter-of-factly. "He has been since birth. You've lived in the City and this will be hard for you to understand, but when I discovered he'd be born blind, I couldn't terminate the pregnancy. I made a choice."

"You knew he was like that before you left? You abandoned me for a defective?" I gaped at her. I pulled my hands back and shifted away from her.

"No! I made a choice to leave with *both* my children. You were supposed to follow. You and Sy. I thought we'd all be together. I never expected—" she broke off. "Sixteen years I've waited for you!"

"Why didn't you terminate the embryo? The tests would have shown something was wrong. You were still young, you could have carried another. What was so special about that one?"

Mara gave me a sad smile. "I have so many things to tell you," she sighed.

"Sy's healthy too, there was no reason—"

"He's not Sy's child."

Her words silenced me.

"This pregnancy was part of a special project. When the Scientists built the City, it was a short-term solution. One generation, two at most, would be housed under the dome. But after decades, it was obvious the longer we stayed in the City, the harder it would be to leave. How could a people who had only known life in the City survive outside? That was the question I was working on. We needed to study the Prims and see if there was something different about them, some kind of genetic mutation that made it possible for them to survive outside. So many people had died before, during the droughts and floods, what if there was something special about the Prims that had allowed them to survive all those disasters too?"

"Survival of the fittest," I whispered under my breath. We'd learned about it in school. It helped explain the need for balancing and the genetic testing of embryos.

Mara nodded. "We needed to find ways to make Citizens stronger. We called it Genetic Intertwining. A Prim's DNA was extracted and used to fertilize the egg."

Sepp was part-Prim? I blinked, making sense of it. My hand flew to my mouth. "The two hunters! The ones the City captured. Ezekiel was telling the truth!"

Mara's face darkened. "Yes. I was Project Leader, so it only seemed right that I should be the first carrier." Her face twisted with guilt. "I wished I'd known the impact of that decision."

"You kept them as prisoners?" I couldn't imagine this woman, my *mother*, involved in such a sinister plan. I'd thought the Prims were the ones to be feared, but Gideon, Akrum and Ezekiel were right: it wasn't them. It was us.

Fresh tears fell down Mara's cheeks. "You can't tell anyone here, Kaia. If they knew," she broke off and shook her head. "They think I was forced to take part in the project, the same as the Prims."

"You lied so they'd take you in," I whispered. "What would they do if they knew the truth?"

She shook her head, her chin quivered. "I don't want to think about it."

My chest tightened at her words. "But it was all a waste. The experiment failed. Sepp's a defec—blind."

"It didn't fail," Raina said with a shake of her head.

I stared at her, my breath caught in my throat. I knew what she was going to say before the words left her lips.

"Sepp wasn't the first attempt. You were."

Lev

I'd drunk both canteens dry trying to decide what to do. Guilt over Raf's death raged in me. I wanted to believe it was outside that had turned me into a monster. A murderer.

The hormone surges left me weak. I couldn't think straight. One minute I was tearful with remorse, and the next angry at

Raf for threatening me. In lucid moments, I knew I couldn't stay on the rock forever, no matter how much I wanted to. I needed a plan. I needed to find Kaia. And I needed more water.

Picking up the canteens, I slung them both over my shoulder and rummaged through Raf's pack to find extra food. I had enough now to last for days. I held the knife in my hands and shimmied down the slanted trunk on all fours, alert for the beasts.

Every time we'd seen the beasts, it had been by the stream. I couldn't risk another encounter with them. I didn't stop to fill my canteen, but moved further into the forest. Maybe Kaia had made the same choice and that was why we hadn't found any evidence of her.

Or maybe the Prims found her? Or the beasts?

I tried not to think about either of those things as I hiked the pack up on my back and got swallowed up by trees.

The sun had risen higher in the sky when my boot squelched into the ground. Not too far away, a waterhole was hidden in the trees. It wasn't tumbling over rocks, like the stream, but sludgy and still.

Had Raf said something about not drinking from stagnant pools of water? I didn't care. It was water and I was thirsty. More than thirsty. My mouth felt like the parched valley floor before the storm came. I couldn't be bothered with filling the canteen. I put my chin right down to the water and splashed handfuls into my mouth. After I'd drunk so much I thought my stomach would burst, I let the water gurgle into the canteen. My head was clear. Without Raf, I didn't have competing ideas. I could focus on finding Kaia and making sure she was safe. And then, together, we'd decide what to do.

An unfamiliar odour carried on the wind. Not the woodsy smell of damp trees I'd grown accustomed to, but something warm and heavy. Raf had told me about fire, how it had been used before for heating and cooking. He'd never built one, but the Prims used them. They didn't have energy sources like we did in the City. Was this the smell of smoke he'd told me about? I lifted my head, breathing it in. The breeze shifted and the scent was gone.

Somewhere, in the distance a beast howled. A long, mournful cry that made my skin prickle.

⌒

I must have walked for hours. Everything looked the same. Wiping sweat from my brow, I tried to focus. Trees swayed and floated in front of me, multiplying into two and then four. I stumbled back to the stream by accident. The threat of beasts wasn't as great as my need for water. Was it being untethered that made my stomach churn? Or the sounds of the beast feasting on Raf that echoed in my head? I stumbled to the stream and dipped my empty canteen in the water.

A crashing in the forest on the other side of the stream made me jump. *The beasts are coming*, a voice echoed in my head. I dashed behind some trees, tucking myself out of sight. Even if they couldn't see me, they could smell me. I heard the beasts sniff the air. They looked to where I hid, yellow eyes glowing in the murky forest light. One growled, baring its fangs, and I crouched lower. *It can see you.* My heart pounded against my ribs.

A howl deeper in the forest made them both turn and lope away. I stayed where I was, too scared to move.

Kaia

All I could see was a pinprick of light. Raina, who was now Mara, hovered over me.

"Kaia?" From somewhere far away, her voice echoed. "Kaia?"

I ignored it as thoughts hammered in my head.

I am part-Prim.

I was abandoned for a defective.

I should never have left the City.

Mara grasped my shoulders, forcing me to turn towards her, but I jerked away. "Don't!" I said. A jolt of anger surprised me. "Don't touch me." I glared at her. "I came to find you. I thought—" And then I realized since leaving the City, all I'd thought about was surviving and getting to the Prims. I'd never considered what would happen next.

"I thought you'd be someone else." It was clear then, who I'd been looking for. I'd left the City to find Mae. But Mara wasn't Mac. Mae would never have deserted me. Not for a defective.

A look of pain crossed Mara's face. "I know it must be hard finding out the truth."

I frowned at her, my emotions dangerously close to the surface. "My whole life was a lie! Sy knew and never told me." My voice dropped, "Did Mae?"

Mara opened her mouth to explain, but I didn't let her.

"Do you know I've spent my life studying Sy, looking for some resemblance between us." Tears welled in my eyes. "When I should have been in the underland, trying to find a *Prim!*" A wave of distaste rose in me. "And you!" I rounded on her, anger and hurt spilling out of me. "You left me to save *him?* A half-breed defective?"

"No, Kaia." She shook her head, her face pinched and determined. "I left to save you. By the time I realized Sy wasn't coming, I had no choice. I had to get to the Mountain. Do you know what they would have done to me if they'd realized I'd tried to leave?"

I sat staring at her, trying to make sense of what she told me. I wanted it to be true, to believe that she'd never meant to leave me in the City. Never meant to choose an unborn defective over me. But I was reeling, falling into darkness again, the revelations too shocking to comprehend.

"Not a day has gone by in sixteen years that I haven't looked out to the valley and thought of you. I knew, one day, you would come." Mara pressed on. "If I could have gone back to get you, I would have."

The sharp edge of distrust cut through me like a knife. I wanted to run and hide until I could sort my feelings out, but I had nowhere to go. I'd risked everything to escape to the Mountain. *Had I made a mistake?* The tears in my eyes overflowed, clinging to lashes and then rolling down my cheeks.

Mara inched closer on the cot. The salt of my tears mingled with the musky scent of her. She reached out to stroke my cheek, her finger pausing at the implants by my ear. Small lumps under the skin that connected the pulse point to my brain and marked me as a Citizen. "I promise, I'll never let you go again, Kaia," she whispered.

I wanted so badly to believe her, my heart ached. "I need to sleep," I croaked and shifted my head away from her touch.

Mara nodded. "I have to leave for a while. There are people I need to check on. I'll be back soon. Get some rest," she murmured. She took a basket of supplies and let the door thud shut behind her.

When I woke up, Mara was still gone. The door softly bumped against the threshold, keeping rhythm with the wind outside. Sunlight filtered through the windows, shedding murky light on the odd assortment of jars and containers that lined the shelves. I looked around. Mortar and pestles, crude knives and chopping blocks all sat on a table under the window. A dented, tarnished pot hung from a hook on the wall and on another shelf, some chipped bowls and cups.

They were scavengers, searching the Mountain for anything they could use. Their homes were a collection of artifacts. I could identify a few curiosities from Mae's stories. Three books sat perched on a shelf, their covers disintegrating and pages yellowed with age. I peeked out the window. Sepp and Gideon sat on logs around the fire while Mara stirred what was inside a metal pot. She said she'd been waiting for me, but she'd made a life without me. She'd lied about what she'd done in the City, hiding who she was. What kind of a person was she, really?

I went back to the cot and lay down. I couldn't go outside and sit with them, talk to Sepp as if he was normal, accept him as my brother. I pulled the blankets over my head and waited for sleep to come, a welcome reprieve from the anger and hurt that swirled dangerously close to the surface.

I woke to the bang of the door and the smell of food. Mara stood beside the cot with a bowl of soup in her hands. "I thought you might be hungry," she said and set a bowl and wooden spoon down on the table.

Sliding the covers back, I planted my feet on the floor and tried to stand. But the room swayed and I had to sit down again. My knee didn't throb anymore, but it was stiff and sore.

"I changed the dressing on your knee," Mara said. "It's healing well."

"It's not infected?"

Mara shook her head. "Things that would kill a Citizen won't affect you the same way. Look," Mara bent down and untied the bandage. The cut underneath was covered with a strong-smelling paste, green and grainy. She wiped it off to show me how it had healed. "The other Citizens wouldn't have survived a cut like that." She pointed to the insect bites that covered my arms. "And mosquito bites could kill them. Or bacteria in water. Heatstroke," Mara shook her head. "So many things."

"You survived," I pointed out.

Mara nodded. "My training helped. I was careful. I brought medicines with me from the City to fight infection. I'd studied plants, I knew which ones could help. Over the years, my immunity has improved."

I watched her warily as she tied the cloth around my knee. "You should eat."

Heat from the soup radiated through the wooden bowl. I tasted a spoonful and grimaced, surprised by the sharp taste. "We flavour our food with oregano and garlic," she said, watching my reaction. "It grows wild out here."

I nodded and tried another bite. Chunks of sweet potato, corn and carrot floated in a dark broth. Each bite was a different explosion of flavor. Sweet potatoes in the City were bland, but these popped and the carrots tasted rich.

"Did you like it?" Mara grinned as I drank the last drops of broth.

I nodded.

"Sepp made it," she said.

His name left a bitter aftertaste. I put the bowl down and wiped off the last drops of liquid with the back of my hand. "He can cook?" I asked.

"Yes. Of course."

Tears prickled in my eyes at the sharpness of her tone. I rubbed the pulse point in my finger. The raised bump in my skin was the only tangible memory of the City.

How long had I been gone? Three days? My escape and the journey across the valley seemed like a dream—foggy and distant. And out of my hazy memory, two figures I wanted to forget emerged. The overseers.

Was it possible they were still on the Mountain? I stared at the pulse point on my finger. I'd had the chance to tell Ezekiel about them and I hadn't. What would he do if I admitted I'd lied to him? Beat me like he had Rufus? Throw me out of the camp? I'd have to go back to the City and live as a prisoner. But before I could get anything out, there was a commotion outside. Gideon and Sepp were shouting and there were other voices too. Mara turned and flew out the door.

"Come out, refugee!" someone yelled.

I peeked through the window and counted six people standing across the fire from Sepp and Gideon. One of them was Nadia. A few of the males had long sticks sharpened to a point. I ducked down, but felt ridiculous. Obviously, they knew I was in Mara's dwelling, otherwise why would they be there? I looked around for something I could use to defend myself. A knife, its blade like a cleaver, lay on a cutting board. I grabbed it and tucked it up the sleeve of my shirt.

"We know you're in there!" one of the males called.

I pushed the door open and tried to look as intimidating as I could. Gideon and Sepp were standing now. There wasn't much Sepp could do to help, but I appreciated the scowl he gave in the direction of their voices.

Gideon frowned at the Prims. "Here she is. What do you want with her?"

"She's not welcome here," Nadia said.

Maybe I should have been scared. After all, they'd come armed and showed no signs of backing down. But I had Gideon and Mara on my side. And I knew I'd done nothing to deserve their animosity.

Nadia should have given classes on glaring techniques. She fired a scathing look in my direction that made me flush. "City people don't belong on the Mountain. You're feeding her and giving her clothes and medicine and you don't know anything about her. You're both letting her sleep in your shelters!" She held up her spear and pointed it accusingly at Mara and Gideon.

"After all the City's done to us, we shouldn't be protecting the refugees, we should be throwing them to the beasts."

A storm of anger brewed in me. I'd done nothing to the Prims. Her hatred was unfounded. Mara clutched my hand and I bit back the words I wanted to shout at Nadia.

"I'm not the only one who thinks this way. I'm just the only one willing to say it to your face." Nadia continued. There was grumbling approval from the others, including two young males with the same coppery orange hair as Nadia. They must have been the brothers Gideon had told me about.

Mara came to my defence first. "Kaia had nothing to do with what happened to your father. She wasn't even born when he was captured."

I gave her a sidelong glance. How could she look Nadia and her brothers in the eye knowing their father had been her captive?

"She's one of us, you know. She's part-Prim, like me," Sepp spoke in her direction and his words silenced all the mutterings. "It's how she's survived outside of the City this long."

Nadia's face flushed a dark red. She turned her glare to Mara. "Is it true?"

Mara nodded. "She was the first. There were no aberrations so she was allowed to live as a Citizen."

Nadia glowered. "Part-Prim doesn't make you one of us. You're still from the City." Her words were laced with contempt.

"Why didn't she leave with you?" One of Nadia's brothers asked the question, but the way Gideon listened, I could tell he'd been wondering about it too. Mara had told them her mate had left with her, so the truth about Sy couldn't be used. Mara opened her mouth, but nothing came out.

"Mae," I blurted. "She left me with my elder, my grandmother. As she aged, she'd need someone to energy-share with her, or she'd be balanced."

Mara squeezed my hand in gratitude.

I took a step closer to Nadia and met her gaze. I'd never condoned what the City had done. I hadn't even known about it until Mara confessed the truth. The City had too many secrets and I didn't want to be part of any of them.

"I left the City because the Council gave the order to balance my grandmother. Losing her was the hardest thing I've ever gone through. Harder even than escaping and getting to the Mountain." I paused. Sepp, Gideon and Mara were listening too. "I couldn't stay in the City without her. That's why I came to the Mountain. I keep wondering, what's worse? Knowing a parent and losing them, or never knowing them at all?"

"You expect us to feel sorry for you?" Nadia asked. The Prims flanking her didn't look as hostile, though one of the females frowned as I spoke.

I shook my head. "No. We have more in common than you think. We've both been wronged by the City." There was a long pause. Nadia's brothers looked uneasy, waiting for their sister to say something.

Mara broke the silence. "Would anyone like tea?" she asked, her voice shrill with nerves.

Nadia snorted and shook her head. "I'll never sit at a fire with her." She turned on her heel and marched away from Mara's hut. The rest followed her.

Mara shook her head after Nadia. "Don't take it to heart. She's had a hard life. After her mother died, she had to look after the boys. I think deep down, she's waiting for her father to return."

"How can I not take it to heart? She hates me. And she's poisoning others against me too."

Gideon gave me a somber look. "Letting Mara remove your pulse point would help. If the others saw you were ready to take it out, it would make it easier for them to trust you."

I wondered if giving up my old life was the right choice. I didn't know if I could go back to the City knowing what I did, but Mara wasn't the person I thought she'd be. Was living as a Prim the life I wanted? What if Gideon was wrong? What if I removed my pulse point and they still didn't accept me as one of them?

My head swam with indecision. "I'll think about it," was all I could say. "Thanks for the soup," I said and made my way back to Mara's shelter. Curling up on the cot, I let their whispered conversation float me back to sleep.

Lev

I woke with a start, jolting to consciousness. Then, I was falling. I landed with a thud on the ground, the wind knocked out of me. I rolled over to my back and groaned.

I looked up into the tree above me. In a foggy memory, I remembered being too scared to sleep on the ground, fearful of the beasts. A quick zap of static shot through my ear. And then I felt it, barely discernible at first. My pulse point was beating! I held it up in the shadowy light of the forest. After days of being untethered, I was connected again. From the tip of my finger, the hologram appeared.

A cramping pain ripped through my stomach. I doubled over, sweating, then turned and vomited. When I looked back the hologram was gone. "No!" I shouted. Holding up my finger, I willed the hologram to appear again but the air in front of me stayed empty. I held up my finger again and again, but the beat of the pulse point was gone. Maybe I'd imagined it. My senses, along with my body, were failing me.

It was hopeless. I was sick and alone. Raf was dead. I had no way of finding Kaia. She could be anywhere on the Mountain. Tar had said to do whatever it took to survive, but I didn't know what that was. How could anyone survive out here?

I looked around the forest scanning the trees for movement. That's when I saw it, a stack of stones shaped like a human. It had two legs standing firm on the ground and a long rock for a body, topped with a rounded stone for the head. It was a sign. Behind it was a path, cut into the forest. A wave of relief washed over me.

Just getting to my feet sapped me of energy. I staggered past the stone figure and lurched from tree to tree. My stomach rolled. Dizzy spells and nausea made it hard to walk without tripping over roots. When I came to a fork in the path, another stone man showed me the way. I clutched my knife in my hands, willing myself to be ready for what lay ahead of me.

◠

I pulled myself up to all fours and then stood on weak legs. A wave of dizziness washed over me. I collapsed to the ground. My head spun and I ached with hunger. Every limb was weak and trembling with exhaustion.

Kaia. A hazy memory of her floated into my mind. I needed to find her. I didn't remember why. I *wanted* to remember why and slapped my forehead, trying to beat it into my head. She was why I'd come outside. I stood up and stumbled towards the tree, resting against it. Not far away was water. I could smell it. Moving towards it, I fell on my knees, cupped my hands and scooped up what I could.

My reflection shimmered in the water. I looked nothing like I had when I left. The outside was eating away at me. I was becoming a hybrid like the beasts. What state would I be in when I returned to the City? Could I go back there? I'd have to face Tar knowing what she'd done to Kellen. And worse, knowing what I'd done to Raf. Raf had accused me of being too soft, too much like Kellen. I snorted out loud. Raf's death showed the horrifying truth: I was more like Tar. My stomach turned. The water I'd just drunk spewed onto the ground.

Tar couldn't have known that sending me outside would do in days what she'd been trying to do for years, but that was what had happened. Tar's DNA had surfaced. I was as much a monster as she was.

Kaia

When I woke up, it wasn't Mara in the hut with me, but Sepp. I hugged the blankets tighter, startled. "You're awake," he said, tilting his head in my direction.

I nodded, realized the futility of that, and cleared my throat. "Yes."

"Ma asked me to *watch* you." He smiled at his joke.

He came closer, feeling for the chair. When he found it, he used his hands as a guide to find the back and then the seat. "I made something for you." He reached into a pouch at his waist and pulled out a cord. Hanging from the bottom of it was a whistle, like the one he'd made for Gideon. "Here. Take it."

I reached out for it. "Thank you," I murmured.

"It's a raven," he said. "Ezekiel thinks they bring good luck."

"It's like the one in the place where the elders meet."

He nodded. "Do you have them in the City?"

"No. All our birds are small. We need them to pollinate the plants and eat insects." I studied the carving, remembering the bird that had attacked me. "I saw a bird even bigger than the raven when I was in the valley."

He nodded. "A desert hawk. They're hunters."

"How do you carve them if you've never seen one?" I asked.

"I've touched them, dead ones anyway. My fingers remember."

I put the cord around my neck and brought the whistle to my lips. Three holes on the tube made the same high-pitched noise as Gideon's had.

"If you're in danger, blow the whistle."

"Thank you," I said again.

"What do you look like?" The abruptness of his question caught me off guard. I'd never had to describe myself before. The way I looked now was different than the version of me that had existed in the City. "Is your hair long like Ma's?" he asked.

"No, it's short. And curls around my face."

He smiled at this. "Short?"

"In the City, we don't wear our hair long. It gets harvested for other purposes, sometimes woven into twine."

"And your eyes," he prompted.

"Blue."

"Blue," he repeated with wonder. "Blue is cool, like water. What about the rest of you?

"I'm thin, like everyone in the City. My nose is sort of big for my face, I've never liked it. It looks a lot like yours."

Sepp laughed. "You think my nose is ugly?"

"It looks better on you."

He held his hands out, chest height. "Can I touch your face? It helps make a picture in my mind."

I hesitated, and in the brief moment of silence, his face fell. "Never mind."

"No, it's all right." I said and braced myself for his touch.

Sepp's fingers came towards my face and I held my breath. He started at my temples, running them down towards my jaw-bone. "You have cheekbones like Ma," he said with a smile. "And your nose, it does feel like mine." I sat still while he finished his examination, the warmth of his fingers leaving a trail on my skin.

The door on the hut opened and Mara appeared. Her eyebrows shot up in surprise and then her face broke into a delighted smile when she saw the two of us sitting so close.

Sepp's hands dropped to his lap.

"What do you think? Does she look like you?" Mara asked Sepp. He gave a shy smile. "More like you," he replied.

She sat down and stared at us in astonishment. "Here you are," she said, and her voice broke. "Both of you, with me. It's—it's more than I ever hoped for." Mara's smile was genuine. With all my heart, I wanted to believe her. For a fleeting moment, I saw a flash of Mae in the tilt of Mara's head and the way her eyes crinkled. I waited for the sharp sting that thinking about Mae usually brought, but it didn't come.

Maybe I *could* make a life here with the Prims. It would mean letting go of my ties to the City and accepting Sepp—not as a deviant, but as a brother. I wouldn't just have to see past Mara's lies, I'd have to help her keep them.

Lev

I'd dragged myself as far down the path as I could before the night had closed in on me. A pit at the foot of a dead tree had become my refuge. I lay curled up like a bug and every hour that went by left me weaker. In one hand, I clutched my knife and in the other I held my lightstick. It kept fading. I was too weak to produce enough energy to power it.

In the stillness, I felt my pulse point start to beat. The static of the newsfeed filled my head. I thought it would buzz and then fade away like the other times. Instead, the reception grew clearer. I held up my finger and the hologram appeared. There was a message from Tar.

"Tar," I whimpered. She'd found me.

Her image spoke to me. "You are ordered to return at once. We have sent another team out to continue your mission. Failure to comply will result in punishment." The loop ran through her words again. I drank them in greedily, they filled my head.

The loop stopped and Tar was at her desk. Her dark eyes sliced into me and her voice wavered. "Lev? Lev? Are you there?" For the first time in my life, I saw her look anxious. Did she regret sending me out here?

"Yes," I choked. "I'm here!" I scrambled up, leaning towards her hologram. But she couldn't hear me.

"If you are, come back."

I choked on a sob as the image cut away.

Kaia

It was my third day in the Prim camp and a degree of normalcy had descended on Mara's hut. She returned to her usual routine and spent a lot of the day checking on people. Rufus, for example, needed his dressing changed. She brought other people medicines she made at the work table in her kitchen. When a patient came to her, I'd excuse myself and wait outside to give them privacy.

"You could take inventory," she told me as she ground dried herbs with the mortar and pestle. She'd just returned from checking on an elder with a bad cough. "Make a list of anything that's running low."

I looked at her blankly. Without my pulse point, I had nothing to record information. She gave a little laugh and pointed to a piece of charcoal sitting on a shelf. "Use that and a piece of bark," she told me. "Do you know how to print?" Mara asked.

I did, but most Citizens of my generation didn't. We could read, of course, but there was no reason to learn to print since we had pulse points. Mae had taught me by dipping our fingers in water and practising our letters on the floor of our dwelling.

I picked up the charcoal and a rag to protect my fingers. It felt good to have a job to do and the two of us worked quietly until we heard Sepp's voice outside. He burst into the hut, trailed by two girls. "I'm going to the waterhole. Kaia, do you want to come?" The two girls stood behind him, peeking through the door to get a look at me.

"I think I'll stay here," I told him, casting a look at Mara. I still wasn't comfortable leaving the security of the hut. Nadia and her group hadn't returned, but I'd be vulnerable out in the open. "But thanks," I added as an afterthought.

"I saw storm clouds coming," Mara said, going to him. "Don't stay long." She whispered something in his ear and kissed him on the cheek. I felt a pang of jealousy at how easy it was for them to be together. Sepp and the girls had only been gone for a minute when there was a knock on the door. "Come in," Mara called. The door opened and a very pregnant female walked in.

"Aliana!" Mara said. "How are you?"

"Huge!" she said with a laugh. "And exhausted, but otherwise fine." Aliana eyed me with curiosity. I gave her a tentative smile and she returned it. "My daughter, Kaia," Mara said. It sounded funny to hear my name and the word 'daughter' in the same breath.

"Yes, I heard about you," she said shyly.

I'd seen a lot of pregnant women at the clinic. Some got sickly and couldn't eat, but others seemed to enjoy pregnancy. Aliana looked to be in good shape. "Is this your first?" I asked.

She shook her head. With sunken cheeks, but bright, dark brown eyes, she probably looked older than she was. "My fourth."

"Fourth!" I sputtered.

"I know," she moaned. "The littlest isn't even walking yet." But she said it with a laugh.

"And they're all healthy?" I asked.

Mara ladled water into a wooden cup and passed it Aliana. She took a sip and nodded. "Two boys and a girl. I'm hoping this one is another girl," she said with a sigh. "The boys are a handful."

Mara put her basket on the table beside Aliana and pulled out medical supplies she'd taken from the City when she'd left: a stethoscope, blood pressure gauge and a thermometer. I watched as she put her hands on either side of Aliana's belly and concentrated. Then, Aliana lifted her shirt and flinched as Mara put the cool, metal stethoscope on her bare skin. She listened for a moment and smiled. "Strong heartbeat. It's kicking? Still moving a lot?"

Aliana smiled. "All the time."

"Good," Mara said with a nod. "It's your fourth, so it might come quickly. Send one of the children to fetch me as soon as the pains are regular, or your water breaks."

There was no proper clinic for the birth to occur in. Would Aliana really deliver the baby in her own hut? No matter how clean she made it, it would never be sterile.

"I'll see you next week, then," Mara said and helped Aliana to stand.

"Hopefully sooner," she said as she opened the door to leave.

Mara watched her go, a wistful look on her face. "I've known Aliana since she was twelve years old. She's a wonderful mother. You should see her with those boys," Mara shook her head. "Chasing them around the camp, even eight months pregnant."

"How did you learn all this?" I asked as Mara went back to crushing the leaves in her stone bowl.

"There was a healer here when I arrived. She saw the antibiotics I'd brought with me and took it as a sign. She taught me all she could before she died. The rest I just learned by trial and error."

"But they trust you," I said. The secret of her role in the City with the captive Prims sat between us. Despite her deceits, she'd found a way to be part of their community. I thought of Nadia and her obvious contempt for me. Would she ever accept me?

"It took time," she said. "But they are good people." A shadow crossed her face and she met my eyes. A silent reminder of what could happen if anyone found out the truth. Mara stood up and carefully wrapped each tool in cloth before she put it back in her basket.

"What if you taught me about healing?"

Raina stared at me in surprise. "What do you want to learn?"

I hadn't thought that far ahead. "I don't know. About how to make medicines, birthing offspring?" I shrugged. "Everything, I guess." I caught my reflection in a piece of polished metal hanging on the wall of the hut. After three days in the camp, the burn on my face had become less painful and not as red. Dirt had embedded itself into my fingernails and smudges from charcoal blackened my hands and arms. I didn't look like a Citizen anymore—or at least not like the person I'd been when I left.

"I would like that," Mara said warmly. "What was your job in the City?"

"Fetal assessment technician. I—" but I broke off. She knew what I did, I didn't have to explain it.

"That must have been difficult, telling a woman when a fetus wasn't viable."

"Most understood, but not always." I thought back to the female I'd lied to.

"I was so relieved when your fetal assessments came back normal. But then with Sepp, the abnormalities showed up right away."

"Why didn't you terminate it and try again?"

A shadow crossed her face. "By then, the program I'd started had changed into something else. I found out what the Council really wanted to do with the offspring."

The ominous tone of her words sent a shiver down my spine. She wasn't talking about strangers; she was talking about me. "What were they going to do?" I asked.

"Lock you away in the underland and harvest what they wanted. Genetic material, stem cells, antibodies, whatever they thought would make the Citizens stronger."

My hand flew to my mouth as I stared at her horrified. "If I hadn't left—if Sy hadn't made me leave," I let my voice drift off, digesting all that she'd told me.

"I never told Sy all of it. I was too ashamed." Her voice dropped, as if the telling had worn her out.

"The City is full of secrets. If Citizens found out the truth—" I shook my head with disgust.

"They'd do nothing. The Council keeps them fearful. People are easier to control when they're scared."

"What if there are more people like me? What if the Intertwining Program continued after you left?"

A pained look crossed Raina's face. "It's possible. Jacob and Noah were still there when I left."

"If there were more offspring, where would they be?" I asked, but I already knew the answer.

"In the underland, I guess. Living like prisoners."

Jacob. The underland. In the storm of memories swirling in my head from the day I left the City to my reunion with Mara, something emerged. A name that would have gone forgotten.

"When Sy and I were in the underland, we heard an argument about a child between an overseer and a man. The overseer called him Jacob."

"Jacob," Mara whispered and shut her eyes. "All these years living as a prisoner."

"But the overseer didn't speak to him like he was a prisoner. It sounded like he was one of them."

Mara frowned. "Jacob hated them, what had been done to him and Noah. For a long time he hated me. Until—" Mara broke off.

"Until what?"

But she shook her head. "I've already told you more than I intended."

Without realizing it, she had made it impossible for me to go back to the City. If I did, I knew the future that awaited me. But it also answered another question that had plagued me. "That's why the overseers came after me," I said aloud. After being in the Prim camp so long, I'd given up on the overseers ever finding me.

"What overseers?" Mara asked, frowning.

"I saw them just before Gideon and Akrum took me. They were in the valley."

Her eyes opened wide and she gasped. "Oh, Kaia," she stood up and began pacing the hut. "Where were they? How far away? Did they see you?"

"They'd have found me by now if they could track me," I told her. "My pulse point is broken, remember?"

"Why didn't you tell someone? Akrum or Gideon?" She rubbed a hand over her face and shut her eyes.

"Everything happened so quickly. I mean, Akrum didn't exactly ask me to join him! I was dragged into a cave. And then I found out I'd probably die and you *were* dead. And then you weren't," I rambled on, the events of the last few days blurring together in my head.

Mara didn't look like she was listening. "We have to tell Ezekiel. The hunters have to be warned. There could be other overseers out there."

I balled my hands into fists. "No! Don't tell Ezekiel! If other Prims find out, they'll turn on me. Ezekiel will be forced to send me back," I cried. "Or he'll order me punished like Rufus!" I stood between Mara and the door, barring her way.

"You've put us all in danger!"

I stared at her. "You keep telling me you left to protect me, well, now's your chance!"

Mara threw her hands in the air. "I'm risking all of our lives by not saying anything!" she wailed. Mara grabbed my hand, the one with the pulse point. "This is what separates you." She shook it in my face. "This stupid microchip! The sooner it's gone, the better." She dragged me towards the table and reached for a small knife hanging on a hook.

"No!" I screamed, trying to wrench it away from her. Maybe I was ready to be free of the pulse point, but not like this, in a moment of anger.

"You have to, Kaia! It's the only way we can be sure."

"Sure of what?" Akrum stood in the door. His eyes strayed from me and down to my hand in Mara's grip. The seconds ticked by as I waited for her to say something.

"Sure that the infection hasn't spread," Mara said, flustered. She let go of my hand and pushed aside a lock of hair that had escaped from her braid.

Akrum looked between us and I knew he didn't believe her. "You need to come to the elder's meeting place. Both of you."

"Now?" Mara asked.

Akrum didn't take his eyes off me as he nodded. "It's important."

A knot lodged itself in my stomach and one thought drummed through my head: they knew about the overseers.

Mara and I walked quickly, following Akrum down the path. I was still reeling from Mara's reaction, but then I realized she had as much to lose as I did. If the overseers recognized her, they'd tell the Prims who she really was. "What's this about?" Mara asked.

"You'll see," was all Akrum said.

The elders sat in the same formation as they had the last time I'd been in the shelter. Gideon was there too, and Akrum sat beside him. We had barely sat down when Ezekiel spoke. "There are overseers on the Mountain."

Colour drained from my face. Mara grasped my hand.

"They were on Two Tree Boulder; another hunter and I found them. They're following her." Akrum looked at me. "I heard one of them speak her name."

Ezekiel interrupted and turned his gaze on me. "I need to know if you were being truthful. Is the thing in your finger broken? Because if it isn't, it will lead them to us."

"I swear, it is broken. It hadn't been working in the City for days before I left. It was how I got away undetected."

"But you *were* detected. They followed you."

"Not because of this," I held up my finger. "They knew running to the Mountain was my only option. There's nowhere else to go."

"We should go into the caves," Josephina said. "And hide." The Prims turned to each other, their faces creased with distress, and began muttering.

Akrum shook his head and held up his hand to quiet them. "I won't hide from them. Anyway, there's only one left now. The other was killed."

"How?" Mara asked. Her face was etched with worry.

"They made camp on the wrong side of the stream. Beasts were tracking them and one fell off the boulder." There was a startled gasp among the elders. "He was attacked."

"The other one's gone crazy," Akrum continued. "He drank from the bog. The stinkwater's rotting him from the inside. He's wandering in circles, talking to himself. But he's on our side of the stream now."

"Should we set a trap for him?" Gideon asked. "Or lead him away from camp?

"If he goes back over the stream, the beasts will finish him," Akrum said.

"That seems cruel," Josephina said.

"They never helped us," Akrum gave everyone a pointed look. "We have no reason to show him mercy."

"It's my fault," I blurted. Mara's fears had been right. "They're on the Mountain because of me."

There was a long pause as no one said anything. Finally, Ezekiel spoke. "It's true. They are here because of you."

I sat up straight, waiting for him to banish me, or tell me I'd receive lashes like Rufus had.

"But you're one of us. Mara has explained that like Sepp, Prim blood is in your veins. You came here looking for protection and for your family. You have both. We will fight to protect you, Kaia."

At first, I didn't think I'd heard him right. I was safe, or as safe as any of them were. No one argued with Ezekiel's decision.

"Akrum, follow the overseer. We won't harm him unless he threatens this camp. But we won't help him either." The other elders nodded in agreement. "If he goes across the stream and the beasts attack, so be it. And if he dies from his sickness..." Ezekiel's voice drifted off, his meaning clear.

"Far as I can tell, he isn't a threat. Doesn't even look like a City person. He's got a funny mark on his face. Like a squashed berry," Akrum snorted.

I froze, not sure if I'd heard him right. "A squashed berry?" I asked.

Akrum mimicked placing a berry on his face and smashing it. My eyes grew wide with shock. There was only one person in the City with a birthmark like that.

Lev. Of course. Who else would they send? Who else had a chance of bringing me back? The only person left in the City who cared about me, and now he was going to die for it.

Lev

I'd survived another night, but every time I tried to eat or drink, I vomited. Most times I made it out of the hole at the base of the tree, but sometimes I didn't. The sour odour of sick filled the air around me. I held up my pulse point hoping for another message. Nothing. Not even a flicker. Had the last message been real, or a feverish dream? It must have been a dream. When had Tar ever shown concern for me? If another team of overseers found me, I'd have to explain what had happened to Raf. "He attacked me," I whispered out loud, the story gaining strength in my head. "Went crazy from the surges."

They'd believe me. I was Tar's offspring. She'd raised a hero. And a villain.

My pulse point flickered to life. Its beat calmed me. I was connected again. Part of something. The City was waiting for me. All I had to do was stay alive until the overseers found me.

Was it the overseers I was waiting for, or someone else? A blurry image of a female stayed on the edge of my consciousness. I knew her, but her name escaped me. And then, it came to me, like a cool breeze, an exhalation. *Kaia.*

Kaia

"You know him?" Gideon asked, but my expression was answer enough. Mara, Ezekiel, Akrum, and the other elders stared at me.

"It's Lev," I said. I couldn't meet their gazes.

"Who is he?" Ezekiel asked.

"He was my friend. It's why they sent him. He wouldn't hurt me. He's not like the others."

"Lev?" Mara said. "Tar's son?"

I nodded.

Mara's eyes widened and she shook her head. "Tar," she muttered. Contempt made her face turn cold. "He can't be trusted. No offspring of hers could be."

The intensity of her voice surprised me. "You don't know him."

"I know Tar."

I wanted to ask more, to find out what she meant, but all eyes were on us. "He's not like her."

"Don't think it's going to matter who he's like," Akrum piped up. "He's half dead."

"Follow him anyway," Ezekiel said. "If he gets too close to camp…" he raised his finger across his neck in a slicing motion.

My knees grew weak and I buried my face in my hands. "No! You can't do that! He talked about leaving the City, about making a life outside. He hates it as much as I do."

Gideon raised his voice. "He was sent to find you. We can't risk it."

"Gideon's right," Mara said. "You don't know what the City's capable of, Kaia."

"I know what Lev is capable of." And I knew the secrets she needed to protect. No wonder she didn't want to help him.

Gideon's eyes turned hard. "Akrum told us he killed the other one. He's gone crazy."

I couldn't imagine Lev as a murderer. I looked around the circle and shook my head. "He wouldn't hurt someone unless there was a reason." I turned to them, imploring. "Maybe," an idea formed in my head, "Maybe he was trying to protect me, to save me from being taken back. Maybe he's a refugee too!" I looked to Mara, expecting her to see reason. "If he's sick, he'll die. Please, you have to help him."

"He's an overseer," Ezekiel said. "Same as the ones who took Jacob and Noah when they went looking for help. Same as the ones who locked our people out and watched them die outside the dome. Same as the ones who created the beasts and then set them free. We fight for survival every day while they sit in the City, safe. No City person deserves our mercy." Ezekiel raised his chin and looked at the elders.

"He's no threat," I said desperately. "He's sick and weak. At least take me to him. I can find out the truth." The thought of Lev out here, alone, searching for me, willing to die for me was too much to bear. "Please!"

Mara shook her head. "It's too dangerous."

"Lev wouldn't hurt me." I ignored a flicker of doubt. He *was* Tar's son. And Sari's mate, I remembered with a bitter jolt. He'd betrayed me once. What if he'd learned the truth about my genetics and planned to drag me back?

A loud gong sounded. One. Two. Three times.

"Enough," Ezekiel said. "We have other concerns."

"What's going on?" I asked. The fire hissed as Ezekiel tossed a bucket of water on it. A spray of sooty water hit my pants.

"A storm," Mara said, standing up. "We wait them out in the cave." I followed her out of the shelter. Outside, the wind had picked up and dark clouds rolled into the clearing, covering the sun. Across the clearing, I saw Nadia. She wasn't scurrying around collecting food and belongings like everyone else. She was staring at me with unconcealed scorn. Did she know why Ezekiel had called me to his shelter?

The gong sounded again. Three more beats. "A bad storm," Raina said.

Her steps quickened as a loud crack of thunder split the air. "Go to the cave. I'll meet you there. I need to get my medicine kit." The rising wind whipped the words from her mouth. Everyone rushed around, barricading the windows on their shelters, pulling cleaned clothes off bushes and hauling baskets of food inside. Commands were shouted and obeyed. Two girls ran into me, knocking me sideways. I recognized them as the girls who had gone to the waterhole with Sepp.

I ran after one and grabbed her sleeve. She turned, panic clear on her face. "Where's Sepp?"

She started to cry. "I don't know! He was beside me and then my sister fell. I went back to help her and he was gone."

I looked wildly for Mara. Across the clearing, she was heading for her hut. "Mara!" I screamed. "Mara!"

"What? What is it?"

"It's Sepp," I said, catching up to her, breathless. "He's missing!"

Lev

My mind swirled from fever and sickness. My legs had grown numb and my back ached. Wispy tendons of roots hung in my face as the thicker fingers stretched, sucking and digging, into the soil.

I was waiting for someone. Who?

The overseers, Tar whispered in my ear.

I turned, looking for her, but she was gone.

No, not the overseers. I was waiting for Kaia. Kaia was coming to get me. I could feel her near me. We'd hide in the hole together.

I listened for her voice, pressing my ear into the hard-packed earth. But it wasn't Kaia's voice I heard, it was the Earth's heartbeat. The vibration drummed through me. I counted. One. Two. Three. And then it stopped. It wasn't the Earth. It was the Prims; they were calling to me. There was a pause and three more beats.

The noise would lead me to them. A sudden elation filled me. I could find them. I poked my head out of the hole. An image wavered in front of me. Kaia. She was there, right in front of me. She tilted her chin in greeting, a smile lifting the corner of her mouth. She held out her hand. *Come with me.* Before my eyes, her image melted into Tar. *Do what you have to survive!* she ordered.

A flush of anger rose in me. I *had* done what it took to survive. I'd killed Raf. I could feel her black heart beating where mine should have been. She'd turned me into a monster. I used all my strength to pull myself out of the hole. Brandishing the knife, I charged at her. "I hate you!" I screamed, slashing at her. But it was air. I flailed at nothing. I was alone.

Kaia

Mara stared at me for a moment in frozen panic. The air shifted, like it was being stirred from above. Gusts of wind bent the evergreens trees as if they were nothing more than bamboo reeds.

"Sepp!" The wind ripped the panicked cries out of our mouths. My shirt billowed around me as I fought the gale that screeched across the clearing. Corners of roofs threatened to fly off as the ties that held them loosened, and they creaked with the pressure of the gusts. All of a sudden, the Mountain shook as thunder rumbled. I stood still, waiting for the ground to stop moving.

Hunched over baskets of supplies, people streamed towards the cave entrance, running and casting worried glances at the sky. Mara clutched each person's shirt. "Have you seen Sepp?" she yelled. Shaking their heads, they tore themselves out of her grip.

"Sepp!" Mara screamed.

Gideon ran from the cave, herding people inside. "Is Sepp in there?" Mara asked.

"I didn't see him." He looked at our panicked faces. "Is he lost?"

Mara gulped back a sob. "We have to find him!"

"The waterhole," I yelled at Gideon. "He went to the waterhole."

Another clap of thunder made me jump with fright. It was like the clouds were colliding in front of me, their anger palpable.

A sizzle went through the air, just before a bolt touched the top of a tree. I heard it crack and the tree split from its trunk, its branches dropped to the ground.

"Get inside!" Gideon shouted, already sprinting away from us, holding his arm up to shield his face from the driving rain. "I'll find him."

Mara turned to me. "Get my kit," she yelled. "It's under my cot. Bring it to the cave. We might need it. I'll get there as soon as I can." Battling into the wind and sidestepping fallen branches, she disappeared from view to search for Sepp. I did as I was told and ran to her hut, splashing through puddles. The door was wedged shut, but with a vicious yank, I got it open and fumbled in the dark for the kit under her cot. The wind hammered at the roof and walls like it wanted to tear the hut to pieces.

Lev was sick, that was what Akrum had said. Talking to himself, wandering the Mountain searching for me. No matter what Gideon or the elders said, I couldn't leave him out there to die in this storm. Grabbing Mara's kit of supplies, I burst back outside as the clouds crackled with electricity.

"Take Mara's kit to the cave," I shouted at a woman and shoved the basket into her arms. She nodded and took off, shepherding two small children with her.

My head was clear. If I wanted to find Lev, now was my chance.

Lev

A few raindrops speckled the ground around me. It was a relief to feel the coolness on my head. Then all at once, the clouds released a thunderous downpour. I crawled back to the hole and dropped in, headfirst like an animal, and then peeked out.

Through the sheets of rain, Raf appeared. "Raf," I breathed.

"Don't leave me." I didn't want to be alone anymore. I didn't want to die on the Mountain. I reached out for him, but he flickered and disappeared. Had he even been there? Or was it the Mountain playing tricks on me?

Raf is dead. You killed him. I spun around looking for the voice. Was it in my head? Or was someone behind me?

Raf darted into the forest toward the stream. Yes, of course! Follow the stream down the Mountain. I could go back to the City. Raf would lead me there. I picked up the knife and struggled out of the hole. The ground was slippery from the rain. I ran to catch up, stumbling and pausing to catch my breath. *I'm too weak.*

Like Kellen, Raf taunted me.

Twice I fell slipping on the wet ground. I had to keep him in my sight, but nausea rolled through me and the forest spun.

"Raf?" I called. I'd lost him again.

The wind picked up and the rain fell harder. I squinted at a figure on the other side of the stream. Raf! I charged towards him, through the swollen stream, determined to catch up.

Thunder cracked the air. Wind yanked at the trees. I shielded my eyes, unsure which way to go because Raf was gone again. *Do whatever it takes to survive.* Tar's voice echoed in my head.

"I'm trying," I shouted. Her eyes glowed at me from the trees. I stared back at them. Had she followed me up here?

No, of course not. It wasn't human eyes that watched me from the darkness. The beasts had found me.

Three of them came out of the trees. Fangs bared, they let loose a low growl. A warning. I held my knife up. The muddied blade looked pathetic against their hulking power.

I tossed the knife to the ground. I wasn't Raf. I couldn't kill one the way he had. I had no chance against three. Covering my head, I bowed down, curling up on the ground, wishing for it to be over, fast.

One advanced, snarling. The end was coming. Death hung in the space between me and the beast. I waited for its claws to pierce my skin, teeth to rip into my body. I could smell it, the stink of its wet, mangy coat. A bolt of lightning lit up the sky. My knife was within arm's reach, its blade washed clean. The beast drew closer. "Kaia," I cried. "I'm sorry." I closed my eyes. Kaia's face, the night we sat in the orchard, flashed in my head. I could feel her beside me and hear her whispered words. *We could live on the Mountain, free from everything and make a life together.*

The reason I was on the Mountain became clear. I had to survive for Kaia.

The beast lunged at me in the same instant as I grabbed the knife. In one motion, I rolled back and jammed the blade into the beast's skull. There was a crack as the bone gave way and the knife slid deep into its brain. Its eyes rolled back, the whites glowing, and then it collapsed, as if its bones had been liquefied.

The other two beasts snarled and ran at me. But I was up, racing across the stream, and my body knew what it needed to do. Get to safety. Back to the pit at the roots of the tree. I didn't look back as I splashed through the water, the other side tantalizingly close. The beasts howled after me.

I saw the path and raced back to the tree. Diving into the hole, I curled up in the corner and clutched my knife in front of me.

There was no sound. No thumping of paws, no snouts poking into the stump, no agitated barking and snarling as they waited outside for me.

Scuttling to the entrance, I raised myself up to ground level and peered out. The storm raged, but the beasts hadn't followed me. They paced on the other side of the stream. I almost laughed, my chest caving in with relief. My legs shook. As long as I stayed on this side of the stream, they wouldn't come after me.

"Ha! Safe," I said out loud.

Too weak to hold myself up any longer, I crouched down, curling my knees into my chest. My head spun. Across the stream, the beasts sniffed at the one I'd killed, urging him up.

I heard a voice, but it wasn't Raf or Tar. My heart gave a leap. *Kaia?* With a groan, I dragged myself to the opening and peered out. A Prim stumbled against the wind. "Help me," he cried.

He was headed down the path. His steps wobbly and tentative. Across the stream, two sets of yellow eyes were trained on him, but the Prim kept walking in their direction, as if he couldn't see them. A shiver of fear ran up my spine. I sank back into the hole. Maybe they weren't real.

But when I looked at the knife, it was still sticky with blood.

Maybe it wasn't their blood. Maybe it was Raf's.

No! I hadn't killed Raf. The beasts had done it. My mind spun with colliding memories. I didn't know what was real anymore. Focus, Lev! I peered out of the hole again.

A clap of thunder boomed and the Prim yelled with fright. "Help me!" he wailed. The beasts stood, noses in the air, growling. He froze, listening. His face contorted in panic.

A cramp in my stomach made me gasp and clutch my gut. My eyes watered from the pain. With a groan of effort, I pulled myself up, clawing at roots and dirt. I had to warn him.

"Who's there?" the Prim asked. He jerked his head around trying to locate me.

"Run! The beasts—"

"Where?" He fumbled with the neck of his shirt, pulling out something and holding it to his lips.

"Across the stream," I answered, but he'd started blowing into the whistle. A sound pierced the air, sharp enough that it made me wince. The beasts whined, jerking back from the edge of the stream, and two of them darted into the woods. One went to its stomach, covering its ears with its paws. The boy blew the whistle until his face turned red, took a deep breath and blew again. The last beast turned tail and ran.

He paused to take another breath.

"They're gone!" I yelled over the rain.

His shoulders slumped with relief. "How close was I?" he asked.

"Close."

He shook his head. His breath came out in panicked gasps. "I heard the gong. We have to go back."

I didn't say anything. He'd lead me to the Prim camp. To Kaia. Another cramping pain shot through my intestines, like they were being wrung out. I groaned, almost falling to my knees.

"Are you okay?" the Prim asked.

"I'm sick. My stomach—"

"Look for the standing stones. There have to be some around here." Another boom of thunder shook the ground, followed by a bolt of lightning. It struck a tree deeper in the forest, the crack of its trunk splitting cut the air.

There were no large boulders, nothing like where Raf and I had camped. The Prim had come through the trees, but off to the side, a narrow path twisted out of the clearing. Beside it, another small pile of rocks, stacked crudely to look like a person.

"There," I pointed. "We have to go down the path."

"Lead me," the Prim said and held out his arm. I took a few steps closer, shivering now. I clenched my teeth against the chills that ran across my body and held onto him. "Don't let go." We took a few steps, rain pelting down.

I gasped as another pain rocked through me.

His hands pawed their way up my arm, to my neck and face. "You're feverish, I can feel it." His brow creased with concern and he brought his hands back to my arm. "What is this?" He touched the fabric of my suit. "Who are you?" The concern had changed to suspicion.

The boy couldn't see, I knew that. Wandering lost on a Mountain in a storm, what were the chances he'd make it back to his people?

I doubled over with pain as another wave of cramps ripped through my gut. I wouldn't last out here either.

"Come on," I tugged on his arm, willing my feet to move. "The beasts could come back." Somewhere nearby, the wind tore a tree from the earth and it thundered to the ground. I spotted a branch on the ground and picked it up, the size and weight made it a perfect weapon. *Do whatever it takes to survive.* The unseeing Prim would lead me to the camp, and then what? I staggered with a wave of nausea. I walked past the stone marker and kicked it over. The stones tumbled onto each other and the boy glanced back, unnerved at the sound, but kept walking. My heart raced with fever or fear. Or maybe both.

Kaia

One word pounded in my head.
Lev.

Forging through the bush, branches scratched my face, tugging at my tunic. I ran carelessly, his name on my lips, desperate to shout it out.

"Sepp!" It was Gideon. He was nearby, crashing through the forest. I veered away. It was impossible to run, the forest was too thick here.

A stone marker at the base of a tree pointed to a narrow, overgrown path. Trees blocked any other route. Crouching low to avoid a branch, I took a quick look back. No one was behind me. Gideon and Mara had gone in other directions, their voices stolen by wind and rain. What if I got lost too? Or they found Lev before I did? I took a deep breath while his name echoed in my head.

The wind grew stronger, whipping the trees into a frenzy. I bowed my head against the rain, holding up a hand to block it from my eyes. The path forked. A stone marker sat in the middle, covered with leaves and debris, as if it had been camouflaged.

"Kaia?" My name, barely audible, floated to me. And again, louder. "Kaia!" Gideon emerged from one side of the path. He was soaked, droplets of water clung to his beard, his hair was matted to his head and his shirt stuck to his chest. "You were supposed to go to the cave!" he shouted over the rain.

The lie caught in my throat. "Not without Sepp." I shook my head angrily. "We should split up to cover more ground." Even as I spoke, my eyes darted through the sheets of rain looking for signs of Lev.

He held my arm, gripping the forearm tight. "No, you stay with me. You don't know these paths like I do."

I jerked my arm out of his grip and swallowed back an argument, desperate to continue my search. I'd stay behind him. As soon as he headed down a path, I'd duck away from him and keep going on my own.

"We're wasting time," I prompted. "Let's go!"

Gideon narrowed his eyes at me. "Are you looking for Sepp? Or the overseer?"

I pretended I couldn't hear him over the storm and shook my head. He shouted the question again, drawing himself closer to my ear, holding my arm tightly. His breath was hot in my ear as he asked the question again.

From behind, a flash of something entered my sightline. Arms raised, it crashed down on Gideon and they both tumbled to the ground. Gideon lay face down and a figure sat on top of him holding a log like a club over his head.

Gideon struggled. "Get off me!"

The figure turned. His eyes, glazed and ringed by dark circles, stared at me, bright with sickness. His mud-covered face was haggard, skin peeling and blistered. But the dark stain on his cheek marked him as mine.

And then another figure stumbled out of the path. It was Sepp. "Don't leave me!" he cried, walking toward us with slow, uneasy steps. "Are you there? What happened? Come back!" he yelled.

"Lev!" I cried, finding my voice. "Let him go."

"Kaia?" Sepp turned to my voice.

"I'm here, Sepp. So is Gideon."

Sepp's face crumpled with relief and he started to sob. My heart lurched at the fear he must have felt in his world of darkness.

Gideon groaned, wincing with pain and rubbing the spot on his head where Lev had hit him. My eyes locked with Lev's and he opened his mouth to say something, but moaned instead and rolled off Gideon. The log dropped and he held his stomach with both hands, writhing on the ground. His face was deathly pale.

Gideon got to his feet. He stared in confusion at his attacker and reached for the log, but I grabbed it first. "What are you doing?" he asked.

I widened my stance, holding the log in both hands. "He won't hurt us."

Gideon's eyes widened in anger. "Maybe not you."

Lev tried to stand. "I thought he was attacking you." His words came out slurred and he only got as far as his knees before he collapsed. Anyone could see he was sick. Dropping the log, I ran to him and slid to the ground. I lifted his head to my lap. His skin radiated feverish heat, but his teeth chattered. "Lev!" I said. "Lev, wake up!'

"He's not going to make it," Gideon said, standing over us. A note of satisfaction in his voice.

"We need to bring him back to camp. He needs to see Mara."

Gideon crouched beside me. His eyes hard. "Ezekiel will never let an overseer into camp."

"An overseer?" Sepp's voice rang out. "But he helped me. He was leading me back to camp."

"No, Sepp. He was using you to find our camp."

Sepp's brow wrinkled at Gideon's words and his face fell. "I led him to us?"

"It wasn't your fault." Gideon moved beside him and rested a hand on his shoulder.

Lev stirred. "Kaia," he whispered. "I'm looking for Kaia."

"Shhhh," I soothed and shot Gideon a defiant glance. "Look at him. He's no threat. Take Sepp back to camp and then find Mara. Tell her I need her help"

Gideon narrowed his eyes at me, his mouth tight with anger. "Please!" I begged.

Gideon grabbed Sepp's arm and left the clearing. In seconds, he and Sepp were swallowed by the sheets of rain and the dark of the forest.

Lev

I felt hands on my cheeks. A voice in my ear. Sweet, urgent. I knew that voice. "Wake up!" she said. "Lev, wake up."

It was Kaia. She stared down at me, water dripping off her eyelashes and nose. I opened my mouth to catch some drops and licked my cracked lips. She looked the same, but different. Every feature was more defined. Her skin had lost its silvery translucence. Days outside had scarred it with pigment. I wanted to slip away again, but she was smiling at me. Smiling and crying. Kaia stroked my forehead. I wanted to go back to the orchard with her and sit in the trees, the smell of citrus fresh and sharp all around us. I closed my eyes again.

Tar floated in front of me. She wanted me to come back to the City. She smiled at me, beckoning. *You're just like your father,* she said, but there was no malice to her words. *You're a hero.* A female stood beside Tar. An elder. It was Mae.

"Mae!" I gasped out loud.

"No, Lev. It's Kaia. We're outside, on the Mountain."

I shook my head, rolling it from side to side till the insides spun. "Mae. Alive."

Her hands froze on my face, cradling it. "She was balanced."

"No. She's alive."

"Lev?" Kaia's eyes dug into mine, full of questions. "Lev! Mae's alive? Lev! Talk to me!"

I couldn't find the words to tell her. They were buried somewhere, hidden in darkness. And then a wave of pain washed over me and everything went dark again.

Kaia

Mara leaned over Lev, her forehead rippled with concern. She pressed his stomach, prodding different areas and then put her fingers to his neck, counting out his pulse. The rain had stopped, but the sky was still a dark grey, the clouds threatening and thunder rumbling in the distance. I was chilled to the bone, shivering in my wet clothes.

As soon as she saw the state of Lev, she'd sent Gideon back to get a stretcher. Made of canvas and two long poles, it rested against a tree. He'd also brought a blanket for me, but I'd laid it across Lev.

She shook her head and sighed, leaning back on her heels. "He needs antibiotics to kill the bacteria in his system. None of my remedies will do any good." Her kit lay beside me. Useless.

"And if he doesn't get any?"

Her silence answered my question.

His face was drained of colour, his lips white and cracked

with fever. He kept mumbling, talking to people that weren't there, the dregs of sentences never spoken.

"Before he blacked out, he said Mae was alive."

Mara gave me a sharp look.

"She was never balanced. They kept her alive. I don't know why. Every time I ask, he blacks out again."

Gideon stood at the periphery of the clearing, but at my words he stepped closer to us.

"He's got a fever," Mara said. "He could have been hallucinating."

"But what if it's true? What if we went back and found her, took her out of the City. Sy too. We could all be together."

Mara's face fell and her hands closed around mine. "Kaia," she said gently. "It's impossible."

"I thought finding you was impossible, but I did it." A flicker of defiance rose in me. I had done it, against the odds.

"Mae wanted you to leave the City. She wouldn't want you to go back for her."

Lev grew agitated and his eyes flew open. He looked around startled, but lucid. "I thought it was a dream," he said.

"No," I said gently. "You found us."

"Us?" He looked at me confused.

"The Prims."

His hand lay open on the ground and I slid mine into it. His fingers closed tight. "Mae," he whispered. "She's alive."

Exhausted already, he shut his eyes. A weak breath rattled through him. "Lev!" I said, desperate for him to tell me more, "Lev, stay awake!"

Carefully sliding his head off my lap, I stood up, shaking the numbness out of my legs. I was wasting time thinking about my options when there was only one thing I could do. Lev would die if he didn't get back to the City. And Mae. Her life lay in my hands. I knew what losing her had felt like. I couldn't go through that again, not when I could stop it. I turned to look at Mara and Gideon. "I'm taking him back to the City."

Mara shook her head. "Kaia—" she started, but I cut her off.

"I have to."

"It's too dangerous. If you get caught—"

"I won't. I'll wait until it's dark and then slip inside the same way I got out," I interrupted her. "I look more Prim now than I used to. Perfect for the underland."

Gideon shook his head. "You aren't thinking clearly. The Mountain is dangerous. You'd never have made it to our camp if Akrum and I hadn't found you."

"I know things I didn't know before." I fished under my shirt for the whistle on its strap and held it out to them. "I know about the beasts and how to protect myself. I'll be prepared."

"With a stretcher, you could do it with another person. But, even using the tunnels, it would be slow going. It would take hours to get down the Mountain, and you'd still have to cross the valley."

I nodded. I knew all that, but wouldn't be dissuaded. Lev had risked his life to tell me about Mae. If he'd killed the other overseer, it had been to protect me. I couldn't let him die on the Mountain.

Gideon looked at Lev with contempt. "He might die before you get there."

I knew he was right, but I stood my ground. Gideon threw up his hands in frustration. "You'll never make it on your own. How will you even carry him by yourself?"

"I'll go." Mara's voice cracked with emotion. She looked as surprised at the declaration as I was.

I shook my head. "No, Mara. What about Sepp?"

"It's only a few days." She looked at Gideon. "He'll be okay."

"Neither of you know the paths to take in the caves. You'll get lost. It's like a maze."

I looked at Lev. "We won't take the caves. We'll follow the stream down the Mountain. Go back to camp and pack what we need," I said to Mara, ignoring Gideon's mutterings. "I'll stay with him."

"Mara," Gideon implored, "you of all people know how dangerous this is!"

But she set her mouth into a thin, determined line and met his gaze. "I let her go once, I can't do it again."

Gideon gave me a long, disappointed look.

"I have to do this," I told him.

He turned and walked toward the forest without saying anything else.

◠

Mara brought a bag of supplies for each of us and dry clothes for me. We lifted Lev's limp body onto the stretcher. A knot of hopelessness started to tighten in my stomach as I thought about the struggle we would face going down the Mountain and then across the valley. But I'd done it once. I could do it again.

I was at the front of the stretcher and Lev's feet dangled over the edge. They flopped as we took our first tentative steps. I remembered Mae's eyes and how they crinkled when she laughed. I thought I'd never see them again, never feel the touch of her hands on my cheek. Was it possible that she was still alive? A glimmer of hope sent a flutter of nerves through me.

◠

A crashing through the forest made me gasp and almost drop my end of the stretcher. We stopped, beads of sweat tickling as they ran down my spine. Mara had wrapped our palms with bandages after they'd been rubbed raw holding the stretcher. It had been a couple of hours and my shoulders and arms burned with exertion. Worse, it felt like we were no closer to the bottom of the Mountain.

"Did you hear that?" I whispered to Mara.

"Stay still," she answered. "It might be beasts."

"But we haven't crossed the stream," I whispered back, lowering my end of the stretcher to search for the whistle buried under my shirt.

A branch snapped and I peered into the trees. It might be Prims. If they'd discovered we were gone, they could take us back to camp. I'd be punished as a traitor. I didn't want to think what they'd do to Lev.

Mara lowered her end of the stretcher. Lev stirred, but was too weak to sit up. I didn't dare glance behind to check on him.

I pulled out my only weapon, Mae's knife, from the belt at my waist. I held it in front of me and tried to look threatening. I hoped I didn't have to use it. "Who's there?" I asked, trying to keep my voice even.

Two Prims emerged and my heart jumped to my mouth. "Gideon! Akrum!" I thought I'd melt with relief. But when I looked at their faces, I hesitated before putting my knife away. "Did Ezekiel send you?"

"We came to convince you to turn back," Akrum said, eyeing Lev.

"I can't do that," I told him. "He needs help."

"Looks like it's the two of you that need the help." Akrum frowned.

I bristled at his words and pressed my lips into a thin, determined line. It had been slow going, but we'd come this far. I wouldn't let him take me back now.

"You think you can carry him all the way back? Just the two of you?"

Gideon looked at me but I stood my ground. "If it's what we have to do, yes." I put my knife back in its sheath at my waist.

He snorted. "You have your mother's stubborn streak, that's for sure." But there was grudging admiration in his voice too.

"We think it's a mistake for you to go back. But if you won't listen to reason, we aren't going to let you go alone," Gideon said.

I was too surprised to move. "You aren't?"

He shook his head. Relief flooded through me when I realized he was serious. With a jubilant laugh, I flung my arms around Gideon's neck. His beard brushed my cheek as I whispered, "Thank you." For the first time since we'd started down the hill, I felt hopeful.

From the stretcher, Lev stirred, a film of sweat covered his skin. He muttered words of nonsense in his delirium. "Kaia!" he croaked. I left Gideon's side and went to him.

"Shh," I whispered, laying a hand on his burning forehead. "I'm here. It's okay."

"We should keep moving," Gideon said. Akrum waved Mara aside so he and Gideon could pick up the handles of the stretcher. "There's a cave entrance a little further down the Mountain. If we take it, we can get to the base of the Mountain before dark and then cross the valley at night. We should get to the City by sunrise, leave him"—Akrum cast a quick glance at Lev—"outside the dome and make it back to the base of the Mountain before nightfall."

His plan could work, especially now that there were four of us, but he didn't know about one key element: Mae. Even if Akrum, Mara and Gideon returned to the Mountain, I couldn't. I had to know: was she alive?

The tunnels sloped steeply downwards and were dank and cold. I shivered and pulled the cloak of fur I'd grudgingly agreed to wear tighter around my shoulders. "Who is he to you?" Gideon asked. We'd just passed the stretcher to Mara and Akrum. I shook the feeling back into my fingers.

"I told you, my friend," I said, looking down at Lev.

"Just your friend?" Gideon asked.

Would he stay with us if I told him the truth? "Yes," I lied. "Just a friend."

Lev groaned, and one arm flinched, as if he disagreed.

We came out of the tunnels at the same place where Akrum had found me. "The stream's just over there. We'll stop for water and rest up." The base of the Mountain was within reach.

"He's flushed. That's a good sign. Means he's fighting infection," Mara said as we took long gulps from the stream. The water dribbled down my chin and I wiped it away. I went to put some into Lev's mouth, but Mara stopped me. "Use his canteen. The water doesn't harm us, but it might not be safe for him."

"Do you think he'll make it, honestly?" I asked, searching her face for the truth.

She sat back on her haunches and surveyed him, frowning. "I don't know," she sighed. "The bacteria is poisoning his blood. Maybe his organs. Even if we get him to the City, it might be too late." Her eyes, so similar to Mae's, searched my face and I knew what she was wondering. Was it worth it?

Twilight made the sky glow powdery blue. I looked at Gideon. His hair lay in damp clumps on his forehead, but his eyes shone bright, as if he was eager for the next part of the journey. Akrum whistled a bird call and smiled when it was answered. They were willing to leave their home and risk their lives for me. A small voice reminded me that Lev had been willing to do the same.

I turned to Mara and the pained expression on her face made me cringe. She was leaving Sepp and her role as healer to follow me back to the place she'd escaped. She was willing to sacrifice her life for me the same way she had for Sepp. But was I willing to let her?

"You have to go back," I said to Mara.

She shook her head, stubbornly, determination flashing in her eyes. "No. I won't let you go again."

"Mara, you have to. Sepp needs you. You are the camp's healer."
My stomach dropped at the words, but I knew they were true.

Her face creased with anguish and she clutched at my hands.
"Listen," her voice cracked with desperation. "Come back with
me. Leave him here. If more overseers come, they will find him
and bring him back to the City."

But I shook my head. "I can't." As much as I wanted to continue my life on the Mountain, I would never feel at peace knowing
I'd let Lev die out here. And Mae. I had to know if she was still
alive. The only way to find out was to go back into the City.

"Kaia's right," Akrum said. "All of us don't need to cross
the valley."

Mara winced with indecision. Finally, she threw her arms
around my neck and hugged me close. I could feel her heart
beating in her chest, the smell of wood smoke in her hair and
warmth of her cheek against mine. "Letting you go sixteen years
ago was the hardest thing I ever did. And now, I am doing it
again. What kind of a mother am I?" Her whispered question
left me breathless.

Shutting my eyes, I fought the tears from falling and clung
to her. Our embrace the only answer I could give her.

◗

At the base of the Mountain, the trees thinned and the valley
stretched out below. The stream carved a path to the City. I
turned to Gideon and Akrum. "Are you sure you want to do this?"

Gideon and Akrum set the stretcher down. "We've come
this far."

Akrum looked around him and picked up a branch from the
ground. "We could build a raft, you know. Tie some branches
together and float him down the stream."

"You've got rope?" Gideon asked. Akrum nodded. "Worth a
try," Gideon said. "Be faster than carrying him."

My back and shoulders ached. Akrum's idea made me want to cry with relief. While Akrum and Gideon went to search for branches that could be lashed together, I bent down to check on Lev. "We'll be there soon," I whispered to him. His teeth chattered and I tucked the blanket tightly around his body. His fever had gotten worse since Mara had turned back.

A jolt like a million pulse points zapped me in the back. I fell to the ground, my limbs useless. Muddled images blurred in front of me. Two overseers. Akrum's body dragged from the trees. And then Gideon's. An overseer holding a stun gun stood above him.

The effects of the stun gun rattled through my body. Saliva dribbled down my chin. "Gideon," I gurgled. It was the most I could get out. He wasn't moving. Neither was Akrum. Had the jolt they'd been given killed them?

An overseer stared down at me. He wore the same suit as Lev and bore the tell-tale translucency of a Citizen. I noticed his eyes though. They were blue. And his body was broad-shouldered and muscular; more like a Prim's than a Citizen's.

The blue-eyed overseer crouched down and pulled me into a sitting position so he could tie my hands behind my back. I gasped as the ropes he tied cut into my wrists. "Sorry," he said in a low voice and loosened them.

I watched as the other overseer used Lev's pulse point to check his vital signs.

"How is he?" the overseer behind me asked.

"Not good." He pulled a vial of liquid from his pack and plunged a syringe into it, filling the cylinder. "I hope this works," he muttered as he injected it into Lev's arm.

My captor pulled me to stand, but it took all my strength not to collapse at his feet. "I've been waiting a long time to meet you," he said softly.

"Oo are oo?" I slurred.

He didn't answer me. Instead, his eyes landed on the knife in my belt. He looked at the overseer behind me and drew the knife out of its sheath. His voice was barely a breath. "I've also been waiting a long time to do this."

He was going to stab me! My heart jumped to my throat. After everything, *this* couldn't be how it ended. But, when he looked into my eyes, it wasn't my death I saw coming. "Duck," he whispered.

In a split second I realized his intention. I bent down as he pulled his arm back and let go of the knife. Not just let go, he sent it with such force that it sailed through the air and landed in the overseer's chest with a sickening crack.

The overseer didn't see it coming. He looked up in shock and gave a strangled cry. "Jacob?" He staggered forward choking on the blood that filled his lungs.

Jacob?

The overseer's legs buckled and he tumbled forward, lying motionless on the ground. Dead.

"You killed him." The thud of the knife entering his body echoed in my head.

Jacob walked to the overseer and rolled him over with the toe of his boot. The overseer's lifeless eyes stared up at him. He bent down, pulled the knife out of his chest and wiped it clean on the dead man's suit. The smears of dark blood were a stark contrast to the stiff white fabric. A swell of vomit rose up my throat as Jacob walked back to me holding the knife. With a sharp thrust, he cut the ropes binding my hands and held the knife out to me. "You'll need this."

I didn't take the knife. I started to shake, and all at once, huge, hiccupping sobs burst from my mouth.

Jacob's face softened. He put his hands on my shoulders and bent his head so we were eye level. His blue eyes met mine. "Do you know who I am?"

"You're my—" I couldn't bring myself to say it. Father wasn't the right word, but neither was birth elder.

He nodded. "Raina told you."

"She's Mara now." My voice was a croak.

"Mara," he let the name roll off his tongue. "So she's still alive." He sounded surprised and maybe disappointed too.

It was my turn to nod. He gave me a long look. "We have a difficult journey ahead of us."

I had so many questions, but I didn't trust myself to speak; there more important things to worry about. I looked around the clearing and stumbled over to Gideon.

He lay on his side, breathing in short, rapid bursts. "He'll be okay," Jacob assured me. "Egan gave him a strong jolt but not enough to kill him."

"And Lev?" I asked weakly.

Jacob's mouth twisted in a scowl. "An injection of freshly harvested stem cells."

My stomach rolled at the word 'harvested' and its implications. Mara's fears for the intertwining project had been real. I looked at Lev and wondered if the medicine would work. Another cruel irony: he'd come to protect me from the thing that might save his life.

I stared at Jacob as he looked across the valley; the City was a speck in the distance. Even if I hadn't been shocked by the stun gun, words would have failed me. He took a deep breath, letting it fill his lungs. "I thought I'd never see outside again. Never stand on this Mountain." The pain of eighteen years in captivity showed on his face.

Jacob sat down and gestured for me to come closer. He twisted the cap off his canteen and passed it to me. "Drink. You'll feel better."

"How did you get out?" I asked, taking a long sip and handing him back the canteen.

"When Lev and his partner didn't return, another team was sent out. They saw beasts and came back, terrified. The Council realized they needed to send someone who knew the Mountain. Who better than a Prim?"

I stared at him, confused.

"They think they've turned me. That after years of abuse I'm loyal to them." The bitterness of his words made me wince. "And they sent me out with this." He pulled up the cuff of his sleeve and showed me a band around his wrist. "A tracking device."

My heart had started to regain its natural rhythm, but my head still spun. I didn't know if it was the effects of the stun gun or all my unasked questions.

"I've worked hard to make them trust me. It's what we want them to think."

"We?"

"The Underlanders." The name hung between us.

"There's more of you?" Just as Mara and I had thought.

He nodded. "The people who built the City were never released. There's hundreds of them, men, women and children. And then the intertwined, Prim half-breeds. All of us are prisoners in the underland." I thought of the calm, efficient City, so clean and orderly, and of the horrors that existed below. "They want to fight, Kaia. They want their freedom."

"Fight who? How?"

Jacob's eyes grew hard. "The Council. The overseers. Some are on our side; they smuggle us supplies and information. They know what the City has done is wrong." He looked at Lev lying unconscious on the stretcher.

Suddenly I was scared for him. What if Jacob killed him the same way he'd murdered Egan? "Lev's not like the others," I told him quickly. "He hates being an overseer."

"That's what Mae told me too."

"Mae! You've seen her?" My heart jumped. It was true! She was alive!

"Lev promised her he'd bring you back."

I started to weep again. For Mae, for Lev, for Gideon, for me and Mara. And for Jacob. For all of us, for the pain we'd endured at the hands of the City.

On the ground, Gideon stirred. "What the—?" He shook his head and winced. "Kaia?"

"I'm here," I said, crawling towards him. "You're okay."

He tried to sit up and saw Jacob. His eyes widened in fear at the sight of the overseer suit. He fumbled trying to get his knife.

I calmed his hands, still trembling from the jolt. "No, don't! It's Jacob. He saved us." Hearing the words out loud made them feel real.

"Jacob?" he repeated dumbly.

I nodded.

Gideon struggled to focus. "Where's Akrum?" Looking around, he noticed Egan's body. "Who is that? What happened to him?"

"Akrum got zapped too. He's lying over there. That," I said, looking at Egan, "was an overseer. Jacob killed him."

Gideon's eyes flew to Jacob with the same horrified look I'd given him.

"He had to," I explained. "It was life or death."

"I'm sure it was, but how did he do it? What's a Prim doing with an overseer?"

Jacob started to explain again and moments later, Akrum stirred. "Gideon!" he gasped and tried to leap into action. His body didn't obey his head and he fell back to the ground and groaned.

"You were hit with a stun gun," I told him. "You need to rest." Akrum rolled over and looked at me. His hair stood on end and his face looked more wizened than before, if that was possible. He reached out for a tree and used it to pull himself to sitting. "I thought they killed you," he said. His voice shook. He took in the scene around him and for the first time noticed Jacob.

"Akrum," Jacob said.

Akrum stared at him. His mouth opened, but no sound came out. "I don't believe it," he finally whispered. His face contorted in soundless anguish and he began to weep. The sobs wracked his body, making his shoulders shake. Jacob went to Akrum, bending over him and holding his head against his chest, rocking him like an infant. Jacob muttered apologies, as if being held captive had been his fault.

"I never thought I'd see you again," Akrum sobbed.

Gideon and I swallowed back our own tears watching them. The reunion was bittersweet. Akrum told Jacob about the lives that had been lost while he'd been held captive. The hardships the Prims had endured: hunger and cold; storms and illness. "We never forgot you," he finished. "Every child in camp knows your name."

Jacob nodded, and took a deep breath, wiping his eyes.

"Why are we waiting here?" Akrum asked. His usual vigour had returned. "We need to get back. Tell everyone. There will be a celebration!" But his energy was short lived. As soon as he tried to stand, it was obvious he was in no state to go back up the hill. He wobbled and then sank back to the ground.

"It's getting dark," Gideon said. And it was true. The sky had shed its last wisps of dusk. Stars glowed, but night hadn't fully swallowed the Mountain. "We can go to the cave, rest up by a fire until we're strong enough to move."

"What about him?" Akrum nodded to Egan, the dead overseer.

Jacob didn't even look his way. "Let him rot."

Jacob and I carried the stretcher while Akrum and Gideon led the way to the cave. "I used to dream about these tunnels," Jacob said. "I'd map out the maze of twists and turns in my head so I wouldn't forget them." He wasn't talking to anyone in particular, but we all nodded.

Lev

"Kaia?" I groaned, opening my eyes. My body felt not my own, but for the first time since Raf's death, my mind was clear. An orange glow flickered off rough, stone walls. I knew I wasn't in the City, but I felt safe and warm. Layers of blankets made it hard to move.

"I'm here," she whispered.

"Where am I?"

"In a cave on the Mountain. We're resting before—" she broke off. I shifted under the blankets to see who she'd turned to look at. "He's awake," she said and then another face appeared. A male in a survival suit.

All at once, alarms rang in my head. Raf had told me what they'd do with Kaia when they found her. "No!" I shouted. Adrenaline pumped through my body. I tore off the covers and threw myself on the overseer. "Run, Kaia!"

The sickness had left me drained and all it took was a flick of his arm to send me reeling. "It's okay!" Kaia shouted. "He's not going to hurt me."

"That's what he says," I spat. "I know what they want to do to you." I narrowed my eyes at him with as much ferocity as I could muster.

"No, it's not what you think," Kaia said. "He's not an overseer."

From the corner of my eyes, two Prims gawked at me. It was worse than I thought. We were surrounded. I got to my feet and held my arms in a fighting stance, ready if they came at me.

"You're going to take on all of us?" The older one asked calmly. There were deep grooves around his mouth and on his forehead. Wiry grey hair stood on end. He snorted, "Guess the medicine worked."

"Stop it, Akrum," Kaia chided. "He's confused. He doesn't know what's going on."

"Who is he?" I asked, glaring at the overseer. "Why is he here?"

"His name is Jacob—"

"The one they took?" The fight drained out of me. I wobbled on my feet.

"You knew?" Kaia gaped at me.

"Not until I was on the Mountain. Raf told me things. The City's not what we thought it was. You can't go back," I told her. "Ever." I worried that I'd shock her with my words, but instead, she nodded.

"I know. We know." Kaia gestured at the males with her.

There was a long, awkward silence.

"I killed Raf," I blurted. "He wanted to take you back and leave you in the underland. I pushed him off a rock and the beasts came. I heard them *eating him*." Just saying the words made the sounds echo in my head. My guts turned with nausea. "And then I got sick. I hallucinated. I thought I saw him, back from the dead. And Tar. It was all her idea, Kaia. Banning energy sharing, taking Mae, the match with Sari, all of it. I think she wanted to make you so miserable you'd do whatever she wanted."

And me? Had she cared at all when I didn't return? I'd seen one flash of compassion for me on a hologram. Even if it had been real, it wasn't enough.

In the flickering light of the fire Kaia looked more Prim than Citizen. And older, as if her time away from the City had aged her by years, not days.

Everyone sat and Jacob passed around a canteen, first to Kaia and the Prims and then to me. I hesitated before drinking from it. The thought of putting my lips where the Prims' had been was repulsive. I felt their eyes on me and knew I couldn't refuse.

The water tasted pure and clean, and better yet, stayed down. I passed the canteen back to Jacob. "I came to the Mountain to find Kaia, but I'm at your mercy now." I grit my teeth and avoided looking at Gideon, the Prim I'd attacked. "I can't go back."

"Luckily you've been sleeping for twelve hours, so we've had time to consider it," the old Prim said. Why did everything that came out of his mouth sound like an insult?

"You're Tar's son. That makes you valuable. You might be her one weakness." Jacob met my eyes and for the first time, I noticed they were as blue as Kaia's.

"But you're also an overseer. How could we ever trust you?" The old one glowered at me.

I met his eyes. "Hurting the Prims would hurt Kaia. And I'd never do that."

"Stop tormenting him," Kaia told them. "You're coming with us." She emphasized 'us' and I felt a flicker of unease, but then she put her hand on mine. For a second, we weren't in a room with Prims, but back in the orchard, planning our future.

Gideon looked at me as if he'd eaten something rancid.

"If you betray us, I will slit you from your guts to your throat and wear your skin for a coat," the old one said and then gave me a maniacal grin.

I turned away, disgusted.

Jacob spoke, "The offer is conditional, Lev. We need you with us when we go back."

I thought I hadn't heard him properly. "Go back?"

"To get Mae," Kaia reminded me, frowning. "And free the Underlanders."

"The who?"

"I told you he didn't know," Kaia said to all of them. "There are people trapped in the underland. The workers who built the City and others like me. Jacob is in charge of them."

"We're getting stronger. We're ready to fight," he said.

"A rebellion." A slow smile spread across Akrum's face.

"We'll raise an army on this Mountain," Jacob said and looked at me. "And then we'll go back. We know the underland and you know the City. You have inside information about the Council. We can work together to take it back."

It was lunacy to agree to their plan. They thought they could prepare a group of people living in the wilderness to fight trained overseers? We had stun guns and a dome to protect us. Who knew what else Tar had access to? Or what she would do if the Underlanders revolted? But when I looked at Kaia's face, I knew I couldn't say no.

Kaia

Lev had rested and eaten. He got stronger by the hour, but knowing what had made it possible, harvested stem cells, turned my stomach. Gideon and Akrum had rummaged through the overseer's packs, marvelling at the City's technology. The lightstick got passed hand to hand until its glare gave me a headache and I begged them to put it away. The rest of the supplies were divided between us. Lev was weak, but he'd make it to camp, if for no other reason than to wipe the smirk off Gideon's face.

I was going back up the Mountain with a heavy heart. Mae was still in the City. Jacob had assured me that she was safe. As long as there was the chance that I was alive, Tar would keep Mae as bait.

"There's one thing I have to do before we set off," Jacob said. He picked up his stun gun and held it to the cuff at his wrist. When he zapped it, there was a sizzle and thin plume of smoke rose up.

We'd talked about Lev's pulse point. Its beat was intermittent. He was dehydrated and without electrolytes, the electrical currents failed, at least that was what we thought. I hadn't told Lev what would happen to his pulse point when we got to camp. But we would do it together. Our connection to the City would be severed, once and for all.

One by one, we walked into the tunnel that would take us back to camp. I let Akrum, Gideon and Lev go first and stayed close to Jacob until they were out of earshot. "Jacob," I said. "There's something you need to know." I paused. He'd been shocked to learn Mara had born a second child by him. What would my next revelation do? "Mara's never told the Prims the truth. They think the City forced her to bear Sepp and me."

An unfathomable expression crossed his face.

"If they find out who she really is, her life with the Prims will be over."

I expected Jacob to understand, maybe even agree with me, but instead, his eyes turned icy. "They stole my life, Kaia. Raina, Mara, whoever she is now, and whatever she told you, she's not the victim." His voice was determined when he spoke. "And neither are we. Not anymore."

Jacob turned to go, but I grabbed his arm, insistent. "Promise me you won't say anything. Not until you've talked to her." Jacob met my eyes. It felt like two rocks grinding against each other, neither of us willing to look away. "No good is going to come from it," I insisted. "Not now."

"People who take from us have to pay, you understand that, don't you? Energy isn't the only thing that needs to be balanced in the City." His jaw clenched and for a moment, I saw the ferocity that lay beneath the surface. Years of captivity hadn't made him meek, they'd unleashed a beast.

I thought of the person I'd been before I left the City and I knew she didn't exist anymore. I had Prim blood in my veins. I had the strength to survive the harsh outside. I had a people who accepted me and a weapon the City couldn't take away: knowledge.

I didn't know what lay ahead for us. We'd round up a group of Prims, and then what? Storm the City? Tame the beasts to help us? Free the Underlanders? But I did know one thing, I wasn't going back as Kaia.

I was going back as a fighter.

The End.

Acknowledgements

Pulse Point began its journey seven years ago when it was rejected from a screenwriting contest. The dystopian world we'd dreamed up was too good to give up on, so we began developing it as a YA book. Through many (and we mean many) drafts, the story morphed into this novel and we couldn't be prouder.

We would like to thank some people who made this book possible.

Firstly, the ladies at Yellow Dog: Catharina de Bakker, Mel Marginet and Stephanie Berrington. Thank you for guiding the book to publication and beyond.

Hart Pollack and Sheldon Nelson.

Paul and Kathy Zubick; over the years, much of the book was written at your Canmore residence.

Thank you to early readers Harry Endrulat, Kathie MacIssac and Erin Wood.

Colleen would like to thank Nancy for always making time to chat about characters and plot lines. I am so lucky to have a sister and writing partner rolled up in one beautiful package.

Nancy would like to thank Colleen for being such a talented and motivating force in writing this book. Your efficiency and endless energy to write so many drafts while always being open to new ideas has been inspiring.